# THE MISSING CHILDREN

## DI KAYLI BRIGHT BOOK 1

### M A COMLEY

JEAMEL PUBLISHING LIMITED

New York Times and USA Today bestselling author M A Comley
Published by Jeamel Publishing limited
Copyright © 2017 M A Comley
Digital Edition, License Notes

This ebook is licensed for your personal enjoyment only. This ebook may not be re-sold or given away to other people. If you would like to share this book with another person, please purchase an additional copy for each recipient. If you're reading this book and did not purchase it, or it was not purchased for your use only, then please return to the site and purchase your own copy. Thank you for respecting the hard work of this author.

This is a work of fiction. Names, characters, places and incidents are a product of the author's imagination or are used fictitiously, and any resemblance to actual persons living or dead, business establishments, events or locales is entirely coincidental.

# ACKNOWLEDGMENTS

Thank you as always to my rock, Jean, who keeps me supplied with endless cups of coffee while I punish my keyboard. I'd be lost without you in my life.

Special thanks as always go to my talented editor, Stefanie Spangler Buswell and to Karri Klawiter for her superb cover design expertise.

My heartfelt thanks go to my wonderful proofreader Joseph for spotting all the lingering nits.

Thank you to Kayli, Donna and Michele from my ARC group for allowing me to use your names in this novel.

And finally, to all the wonderful Bloggers and Facebook groups for their never-ending support of my work.

Note from the author.

Although I found this book extremely hard to write, when I researched the subject the statistics were mind-boggling. In the UK alone, over

140,000 children went missing during 2016. Reading that, I felt compelled to write this story.
If this book helps to save just one child's life it will have been worth all the emotions I went through bringing you this story.
Thank you for reading The Missing Children.

# OTHER BOOKS BY M A COMLEY

Blind Justice (Novella)

Cruel Justice (Book #1)

Mortal Justice (Novella)

Impeding Justice (Book #2)

Final Justice (Book #3)

Foul Justice (Book #4)

Guaranteed Justice (Book #5)

Ultimate Justice (Book #6)

Virtual Justice (Book #7)

Hostile Justice (Book #8)

Tortured Justice (Book #9)

Rough Justice (Book #10)

Dubious Justice (Book #11)

Calculated Justice (Book #12)

Twisted Justice (Book #13)

Justice at Christmas (Short Story)

Justice at Christmas 2 (novella)

Prime Justice (Book #14)

Heroic Justice (Book #15)

Shameful Justice (Book #16)

Immoral Justice (Book #17)

Toxic Justice (Book #18)

Overdue Justice (Book #19)

Unfair Justice (a 10,000 word short story)

Irrational Justice (a 10,000 word short story)

Seeking Justice (a 15,000 word novella)

Caring For Justice (a 24,000 word novella)

Savage Justice (a 17,000 word novella Featuring THE UNICORN)

Vile Justice (A 17,000 word novella)

Gone in Seconds (Justice Again series Book #1)

Ultimate Dilemma (Justice Again series Book #2)

Clever Deception (co-written by Linda S Prather)

Tragic Deception (co-written by Linda S Prather)

Sinful Deception (co-written by Linda S Prather)

Forever Watching You (DI Miranda Carr thriller)

Wrong Place (DI Sally Parker thriller #1)

No Hiding Place (DI Sally Parker thriller #2)

Cold Case (DI Sally Parker thriller#3)

Deadly Encounter (DI Sally Parker thriller #4)

Lost Innocence (DI Sally Parker thriller #5)

Goodbye, My Precious Child (DI Sally Parker #6)

Web of Deceit (DI Sally Parker Novella with Tara Lyons)

The Missing Children (DI Kayli Bright #1)

Killer On The Run (DI Kayli Bright #2)

Hidden Agenda (DI Kayli Bright #3)

Murderous Betrayal (Kayli Bright #4)

Dying Breath (Kayli Bright #5)

Taken (Kayli Bright #6 coming March 2020)

The Hostage Takers (DI Kayli Bright Novella)

No Right to Kill (DI Sara Ramsey #1)

Killer Blow (DI Sara Ramsey #2)

The Dead Can't Speak (DI Sara Ramsey #3)

Deluded (DI Sara Ramsey #4)

The Murder Pact (DI Sara Ramsey #5)

Twisted Revenge (DI Sara Ramsey #6)

The Lies She Told (DI Sara Ramsey #7)

For The Love Of… (DI Sara Ramsey #8)

Run For Your Life (DI Sara Ramsey #9) Coming August 2020

I Know The Truth (A psychological thriller )

The Caller (co-written with Tara Lyons)

Evil In Disguise – a novel based on True events

Deadly Act (Hero series novella)

Torn Apart (Hero series #1)

End Result (Hero series #2)

In Plain Sight (Hero Series #3)

Double Jeopardy (Hero Series #4)

Criminal Actions (Hero Series #5)

Regrets Mean Nothing (Hero #6)

Sole Intention (Intention series #1)

Grave Intention (Intention series #2)

Devious Intention (Intention #3)

Merry Widow (A Lorne Simpkins short story)

It's A Dog's Life (A Lorne Simpkins short story)

A Time To Heal (A Sweet Romance)

A Time For Change (A Sweet Romance)

High Spirits

The Temptation series (Romantic Suspense/New Adult Novellas)

Past Temptation

Lost Temptation

Cozy Mystery Series

Murder at the Wedding

Murder at the Hotel

Murder by the Sea

Tempting Christa (A billionaire romantic suspense co-authored by Tracie Delaney #1)

Avenging Christa (A billionaire romantic suspense co-authored by Tracie Delaney #2)

# PRAISE FOR THE MISSING CHILDREN

"The first installment of a new series, *The Missing Children* introduces a new team of detectives who are led by a female detective, DS Kayli Bright. Their newest case means the unthinkable for the victims' families, and the story is likely to hit close to home for many readers. Though Comley treads familiar investigative waters that her fans are sure to enjoy, this story features several strong supporting characters with fresh backstories that promise to play out in future books, and I look forward to their development as they each use their special insight to crack the toughest cases." Stefanie B., Line Editor, Red Adept Editing

"M. A. Comley writes to the heart of the deeply emotional task of finding missing children and bringing their abusers to justice. Detective Inspector Kayli Bright captures all the heartache and anxiety of this monumental task, but she performs with such determination and conviction, it'll make you wonder: Could any kidnapper escape her?" Amanda K., Proofreader, Red Adept Editing

# PROLOGUE

Sinead followed her boyfriend, Jeremy, through the derelict house with the crumbling walls, shuddering at all the cobwebs dangling from the discoloured ceilings. The wallpaper, what was left of it, dated back to the fifties, and the large bold flower pattern had faded over time. One panel in particular had peeled away from the wall and hung to the floor. "Do we have to go any further? This place is giving me the creeps."

"Where's your sense of adventure? You want to do the same thing every time we meet up, but do you hear me complaining? We're nearly there now. It's not as if it's a big house."

"Thank God. It will be worth all this hassle in the end, won't it?" Her voice came out barely louder than a whisper.

He chuckled. "Believe me, babe, it'll be worth it. I have a surprise for you that you'll be talking about for years to come."

Sinead gulped loudly. She was even more terrified, not just of the creepy surroundings, but because she had a feeling her boyfriend was expecting her to surrender her virginity to him there. She could think of better places than this shithole, but if it meant holding on to him, she knew she would have to put out. She had a feeling he was keen on the new blonde girl in their class; Sinead had caught him staring at her a few times during maths. If she didn't give him what he was craving, he would move on to pastures new.

Jeremy cleared the cobwebs at the top of the stairs. He looked down into the cellar then at Sinead. "Cool, I'd heard there was one down here. I love cellars, ever since I saw that horror film where Dracula lived in a coffin in a cave-like cellar. Looks like we're in for a real treat, babe."

Sinead backed up a couple of paces. "Oh no, I hate cellars. I can't go down there, Jeremy. Please don't make me. This place is creeping me out. My heart feels like it's going to spew into my mouth any second."

"Coward. Come on." He grabbed her hand tightly and began to descend the stone steps.

Sinead dug her heels in, but when he turned and scowled at her, she relented and followed him down the stairs. The stairwell was dark until her eyes adjusted, aided by the light from the tiny window at the bottom of the stairs. Something crunched under her foot, and she glanced down to see she'd just squashed a huge woodlouse. She wasn't about to lose any sleep over that, but the same thing couldn't be said for the spooky depths of the cellar that awaited her. The smell of damp earth hit her nose, making it twitch. *Christ, this guy has a lot to learn about romance if he expects me to put out down here.* "Jeremy, please? It's too scary for me. I don't like it."

He tugged on her arm, refusing to let her go, and continued down the stairs with a grunt of displeasure. She'd heard rumours about his reputation—if he didn't get what he wanted from a girl, he would dump her and move on to the next one. That thought devastated her. She was in love with him.

She bumped into his back at the bottom of the stairs. Although it was good to be on solid ground, she shuddered and glanced around the vast area. Some areas were darker than others the farther they ventured away from the window. Sinead let him guide her, and when he stopped suddenly, she barrelled into him a second time.

"What is it? What have you seen?" she whispered urgently, her heart pounding rhythmically.

"Ssh! Stay here." He let go of her hand, but she grabbed his hand again quickly.

"No, please don't leave me. I'm coming with you."

"All right. Keep schtum and don't piss me off."

"I will. I promise."

They slipped deeper into the darkness. Sinead tried but failed to prevent her body from trembling as they stepped into the unknown abyss. *Be brave. I mustn't show him how scared I am.* She peered into the darkness ahead of them and saw the outline of something against the far wall. *Holy crap, what's that?*

"Seriously, I need to take a closer look. You stay here. Nothing is going to harm you. I'll be three feet away. That's all."

Sinead let out a shuddering breath and nodded. She watched him ease his way into the darkness. Her breath caught in her throat when the blackness enveloped him before her eyes adjusted to the light again.

"What the fuck is this?" he said angrily.

"What? Jeremy, you're scaring me. What have you found?"

"Quiet, let me concentrate. There's something here. Not sure what it is."

Furious with herself for not thinking of it earlier, Sinead reached for her phone and switched on the torch. Jeremy looked her way and shielded his eyes against the light, then they both turned to the object that had drawn his attention. Sinead screamed and almost dropped her phone in her haste to escape the cellar.

"Sinead, come back. It's okay... it's just a sack. Nothing to be scared of."

She halted at the bottom of the stairs and hesitantly returned to where he was standing, barely a foot away from the sack. "Why would anyone put a sack there?"

Jeremy approached the hessian and spun it around. He gasped.

Sinead slid up behind him and peered over his shoulder. "What is it?"

A large red splodge coated one side of the sack. "I think it's blood."

"Oh no!" Tears of frustration misted her eyes, but she rubbed them away angrily. "Do you think there's an animal inside?" The thought of an animal being tortured and thrown in a sack really upset her. She hated any form of animal abuse.

He took another step forward. "There's only one way to find out."

"No, don't touch it. We should call the police."

"And say what? We found a sack with blood on it?"

"Please, Jeremy, don't touch it. I'm scared, too scared for this. We need to get out of here."

"I'm not going until I've had a look."

"That's morbid. It's obvious something is dead in there. I'd rather not know what it is."

He laughed then proceeded to unhook the sack. "Ugh... it's heavier than I thought it would be."

Sinead gulped and took a step closer. She watched as he loosened the knot at the top of the bag.

"Shit! Fuck... what the hell? Get out of here, Sinead. Quick, run."

She didn't get the chance to see inside the sack before he began pushing her towards the stairs. Witnessing the terror in his eyes was enough to tell her that he'd discovered something far more sinister than he'd bargained for. "What was it?"

"Just get out of here. Stop pissing around and move."

Her legs wobbled, as if they'd turned to jelly, but they scampered out of the cellar almost on their hands and knees in their haste to get away.

He grabbed her phone and punched in three numbers. "Yeah, I want the police. I've just discovered a body."

Sinead's eyes almost popped out of her head. She switched off from what Jeremy was saying to the operator. *A body? What sort of body? That sack wasn't nearly big enough...*

He handed the phone back to her and led her through the house to the outside. "We've got to wait here for the police to arrive. Shit! Sinead, it was... it was a child!"

Sinead covered her face with her hands and sobbed. She felt Jeremy's arm slip around her shoulder before she crumpled to her knees in the wet grass. *Who would do such a thing? A child!*

# 1

Kayli Bright let out a relieved sigh. She was happy with her life, finally. She had a fiancé who adored her and a wedding to look forward to. Even though the big event was months away, a sense of accomplishment seemed to fill her with each passing day. Her hand slid over Mark's back. He moaned, still sleepy from their late night and probably a little hungover if the truth be told. It was all right for him—he could stay in bed the rest of the day to recover from his sore head, but she had work to do. Her shift at the Avon and Somerset Constabulary, where she worked as a detective inspector, was due to start in an hour.

"Let me sleep, you wicked woman. Didn't you have enough of me last night?" Mark eased open an eye to look at her.

She flung back the quilt, exposing both their naked bodies, and slapped him on the arse before she ran for the bathroom. "Lazy sod. Hey, let's get one thing clear, Mr. Wren. I'll never get enough of your body."

"That's what I thought. I'll just have another hour or so, and then I promise I'll get my backside out of bed and try to find a job today. Last night, Clive said he might have an opening for me down at the gym. I've got to call in there today to have a word with his boss."

Kayli ran back to the bed and threw herself on top of him. "That's brilliant news, love. I know it's been difficult finding a job since you left the army, but I've never lost faith in you."

He turned over and held her close. She could feel his erection stirring beneath her. "Glad you have faith in me. Mine's begun to dwindle a little lately." He kissed her neck, aware of how much it turned her on. "Time for a quickie?"

Kayli slapped him. "You're so unfair. No, I don't have time. Why don't you pick up a couple of steaks for dinner tonight? I'll leave a twenty on the kitchen table before I go. You never know, we might be celebrating you getting a new job by then."

"Why don't you look after your money, just in case? You know I hate taking money off you. I've still got a bit of savings tucked away. I'll use that if I need to."

"No, that's for our wedding fund."

"Nonsense, twenty quid won't hurt."

She kissed him hard on the mouth, and his arms crushed her to him. Kayli groaned. "Damn, I wish I could stay in bed with you all day, but I have a meeting with the chief first thing."

"What about?"

"No idea. I was summoned late last night and told to report at nine. I need to make myself beautiful. Who knows? I could be joining you in the dole queue by the end of the day." She wriggled off the bed and headed towards the bathroom again.

"Don't even say that in jest. They wouldn't get rid of you; you solve half the bloody crimes at that station. More than the others do put together."

She blew him a kiss from the doorway then stepped into the cool shower. *Damn, I forgot to heat the water last night.*

With Mark out of work, she was doing her best to be frugal without letting him know. Cutting back on the utilities wherever possible, she had got away with it, but as September dawned and the temperatures started to drop, that task was going to be much harder to accomplish. *I hope he gets the job today—it'll take the pressure off for a while, what with Christmas looming just around the corner.*

Her concerns drifted to what she was about to walk into at work that morning. DCI Sandra Davis had sounded strained when she'd arranged the meeting the previous evening. Kayli had wracked her brains to think what either she or her team had done wrong in the past few weeks, but came up with nothing. *Look, there's no point getting worked up or speculating what-ifs. I'll find out in an hour or so, anyway.*

Kayli shivered as she got out of the shower, feeling colder than when she'd got in, not warm and revitalised like she usually did after her morning shower. She brushed her teeth and applied the lightest of makeup before she returned to the bedroom to find Mark fast asleep and snoring gently. She pecked him lightly on the cheek, searched the drawer for her hairdryer, and went through to the small spare room of their two-bedroom terraced home to dry her waist-length black hair. She had no idea why she dried it when all she did was tie it in a ponytail every day anyway. Ten minutes later, she slipped back into the bedroom, gathered her work clothes, and went downstairs to put the kettle on.

After downing a quick piece of toast and a cup of coffee, she left the house and drove through the ever-increasing heavy traffic around Portishead. Her commute to work usually took twenty minutes, but that morning it took her thirty minutes to wade through. Kayli raced up the stairs, bid the team good morning in the incident room, then ran along the corridor to the DCI's office. She arrived with a minute to spare and blew out a relieved breath in front of Fiona, the DCI's secretary.

"Only just made it, Inspector."

"Tell me about it. Damn traffic. Shall I go through?"

Fiona held up a finger, telling her to be patient, and picked up the phone. "DI Bright is here to see you, DCI Davis."

Fiona nodded and motioned for Kayli to go in. She rapped the door with her bony knuckles and turned the handle.

"Ah! There you are. Only just made it. Take a seat."

"Have I done something wrong, boss?"

Davis's brow raised, and she tilted her head to one side. "I don't know... have you?"

"Not that I'm aware of. Sounds like you're annoyed at me, and that's why I asked."

"No, never annoyed at you, Kayli. This lot"—she swept her hand over the paperwork scattered across her desk—"is another bloody story. I wanted to have a chat to see how you're getting on, that's all. Nothing to be alarmed about, really."

"I'm doing well. The team have achieved all the targets set for them at the beginning of the year, and I'm delighted about that. Not sure how that compares to the rest of the station's performance. Maybe you can enlighten me?"

"Not as good as you, apparently, hence all this damn paperwork. You know what? You're the only one in this entire building who truly knuckles down to work when they're here. The others treat this place as a joke half the time. I never hear you laughing when I pass by your office, though."

"Thanks, I think I should take that as a compliment. You know me—I like to give my all when I'm at work, and I think I've instilled the same work ethic into my team too."

"No complaints from me in that department. What cases are you dealing with at present?"

They spent the next fifteen minutes going over the three open cases the team was currently investigating, which included a man who had murdered his wife after he caught her in bed with his best friend. Another case had to do with a new gang who were intent on marking their territory by trying to wipe out the head of the opposing gang ruling the estate. Finally, the third case involved an old lady who had killed her husband who was riddled with cancer. The doctors had refused to give him sufficient painkillers to deal with the pain, and he'd resorted to pleading with his wife to end his life. No longer capable of seeing him suffer, she had agreed to end the pain and the indignity of the godawful disease.

"All these cases are nearing their conclusion then?" Davis asked.

"Hopefully, they should all be wrapped up in the next week or so, unless something else crops up in the meantime."

"Good. Well, I couldn't be more delighted for you and your team. I just wish there were a yearly bonus scheme that compensated those who do outstanding jobs. It might kick the others up the arse then. Sadly, we'll have to plod on, but fear not, your name is mentioned more times than any of your colleagues', positively of course. I couldn't be prouder of the way you tackle your workload. In case I don't say it enough: you're a top-class inspector."

Kayli's cheeks warmed. "Gosh, you've never praised me like that before, boss. Are you sure you're not sickening for something?" she joked, trying to hide her embarrassment.

"Shoo! Go, before I rescind my praises. Credit where it's due. Maybe I'm at fault for not praising you enough or valuing your worth in the past."

Kayli's eyes widened. "I could always do with a raise, you know, what with the wedding coming up next year. All extra funds gratefully received, as my mum always says."

"How are the plans coming along? Has Mark found a decent job yet?"

Kayli rose from her seat. "Nope. He's hopeful he'll have some good news on that front by the end of the day." She shrugged. "If that's all, I better get on."

Davis nodded. "I was just about to suggest the same. Keep me informed regarding your ongoing cases, and let me know when you've completed them."

"I will." Kayli left the office, smiled at Fiona, and walked out into the corridor. She breathed easier as she retraced her steps back to the incident room.

The room fell silent as she entered. Kayli's eyes narrowed as she sought out her partner. "Something wrong that I should know about, Dave?"

"You might need to take a seat first."

Fearing something dreadful had happened to a member of her family, she sank into the nearest chair and placed a hand over her heart. "Go on, hit me with it."

"We've had a call from a couple of kids at a derelict property. It's not good, boss."

Kayli gestured with her hand for him to speed up.

"In the cellar, they found the body of a child in a hessian sack."

Kayli jumped to her feet. "What? We need to get over there ASAP. When was this?"

"Around eight o'clock last night. The kids were messing around at a house."

Kayli frowned and scratched her head. "Messing around? Is that your way of telling me they were about to make out? Why are we just hearing about the case now?"

Dave shrugged. "Who knows what kids get up to nowadays, and I haven't got a clue if they're old enough to be making out. It's our case now because everyone else is up to their necks in work."

Kayli shook her head, clearing her thoughts a little. "So are we... grr... it really doesn't matter. Let's get over to the crime scene and see what we're dealing with. The rest of you, I want you to put an extra effort in to tie up all the open cases within the next day or two so we can give the new one the attention it's going to need. No one likes the death of a child to deal with, do they?"

The two detective constables on the team, Donna Travis and Graeme Chance got down to work immediately. Dave pulled his jacket off the back of the chair, then he and Kayli rushed out of the incident room.

Fifteen minutes later, they arrived at the cordoned-off scene in Tyler Street.

"This place is the pits," Kayli said as they slipped into their protective suits and shoes. "In my day, this part of town used to be the area where newlyweds bought properties because that's all they could afford to get on the property ladder. Some of these places need demolishing. Agh... okay, don't get me started on how the council in this county are letting down their communities."

"I hear you. People are crying out for decent homes around here, but maybe we should leave that conversation for another day." They showed their ID to the constable guarding the house before Dave lifted the tape, they both ducked under it and walked into the derelict shell of a house.

"Why would kids come here? The walls are crumbling, and it's hardly what you would call safe."

Dave raised an eyebrow. "Are you messing with me, boss? Why do you think?"

She shook her head. "That's gross. Maybe it's me getting old or something but the thought of getting it on with a boyfriend in this cesspit..." She shuddered. "Well, would you?"

"Umm... I never had a boyfriend at school."

"You're such a frigging comedian, you know perfectly well what I meant. In the cellar, you said?"

Dave grinned and pointed off to the left. They picked their way through the rubble and litter to an opening that led to a doorway. "Down here."

"Have I ever told you I have a phobia about confined spaces?"

Dave looked at her as if she were nuts. "You sure pick your moments to tell me breaking news like that. Want me to go down there and report back to you?"

While Kayli debated her answer, her stomach did a thousand somersaults and her heart rate escalated. She swallowed the acid burning her throat and shook her head. "I'll see how I go. You first. I'll bolt if I have to."

"Bloody women... scared of a few cobwebs and dark, damp surroundings," Dave mumbled as he turned his back on her and descended the steps carefully.

Kayli let him go a few steps ahead of her before she took the plunge to follow him. To her relief the cellar was anything but dark and confining as the Scenes of Crime officers had flooded the area with lamps.

Pathologist Naomi Stacy was attending the scene. She glanced up at Kayli and Dave as they approached. "Hi, we were delayed getting here, caught up in a major incident overnight. This is a particularly nasty one. I Hope you have a strong stomach this time of the morning."

Dave groaned and shook his head, then he surprised Kayli by making the sign of the cross. She'd never witnessed him do such a thing at any other crime scene. *Not that we've dealt with that many murdered children before, thank God.*

"Jesus! One question—why? What is she? Six or seven at most?" Kayli asked, the bile resurfacing in her throat.

The child was black and naked, very slim, almost too thin, leading Kayli to think that she had possibly been abducted and held captive for at least several weeks.

"You're right. No more than six or seven. She was found in the sack over there. Some bastard tortured her. She has bruises all over her body. Pre-empting your next question, I have no idea if she was sexually abused or not, but I'll pass that information on once I carry out the PM this afternoon. It's shocking… just shocking."

Kayli reached out and squeezed Naomi's shoulder. Naomi had a little girl roughly the same age as the victim. "Maybe someone else should deal with this one, Naomi."

Naomi shook her head. "No way. I want to do all I can to catch the filthy piece of shit. I'd love nothing more than to string him up, dissect his balls and penis one at a time before forcing them down his throat. Callous shit."

"I hear you. I'll join you in that," Dave piped up. He smiled down at Naomi.

Kayli suspected he'd harboured a crush on Naomi for a while, even though he was engaged to Suranne. Maybe "crush" was a little over the top. Perhaps he was just full of admiration for the pathologist, but Kayli had been trying to find the right time to broach the subject with him for a few months.

Kayli sighed heavily. "Let's do what we can to find the shit first. I think there will be a queue outside his cell once he's arrested."

"I think you're right. We'll ensure the CCTV camera in the cell is conveniently broken that day too," Dave said, his fists clenching at his sides.

"Why put her in the sack? Was she kept in there during her ordeal or disposed of after she had died?" Kayli asked, her eyes drawn to the child's body once more.

"Hard to tell at this point. My team will let you know once they've obtained the answers."

"We'll need to know if she was being held here or if her body was dumped after her death. Can you do that, Naomi?"

"We'll do our best. She was probably being held somewhere else and was dumped here. Maybe their intention wasn't to kill her. Perhaps things got out of hand, and the poor mite's heart just gave up," Naomi said, tears moistening her stunning blue eyes.

"Why don't you take a breather? Get some fresh air for a moment or two," Kayli suggested, her own eyes pricking because of the hurt resonating in her friend's expression.

Naomi shook her head. "Her right arm is broken—whether that happened pre or post-mortem, I'm not sure at this point. A quick assessment tells me that she also has a couple of busted ribs. She was treated no better than a caged dog on one of those dog meat farms in Vietnam. Sickening."

"Any form of identification on the girl?"

"Nothing, no jewellery and none of her possessions or clothing were found either in the sack or lying around here."

"Looks like a trip to the Missing Persons Department is in order when we get back to the station. Anything else you can tell us, Naomi? Any skin under her fingernails pointing to the offender's DNA? I know I'm expecting a lot, and in reality, I don't think there's likely to be any sign of that."

"Hard to judge right now. I'll know more once I've carried out all the tests this afternoon. Sorry I can't furnish you with more at this point."

"No problem. We'll get cracking on this one right away. Hopefully, she'll have a match in the missing persons database, and we'll be able to trace the family within the next day or two."

"I'm just going to organise the photos, and then I'll get this precious package back to the lab. I'll be in touch when I can, Kayli. Good luck locating the parents. Tell them to contact me ASAP when they want to see their child."

"I will. Take care, Naomi."

Kayli rushed back up the stairs, with Dave close behind her. Not wanting to contaminate the crime scene, she ran as far away from the house as possible, and emptied her stomach over the overgrown shrubs planted at the edge of the garden. Dave carried on walking out to the car. Kayli wiped her mouth and joined him a few minutes later. "Told you I hated confined spaces."

"Really? I thought it was because of the state the body was in."

In the car, Kayli reached for the bottle of water she always carried with her in the console between them and downed half the contents. "Maybe a mixture of both. Shit! This is going to be the first child's death we've investigated. Let's hope we can do that little girl justice."

"We will. I have no doubts about that. Poor bugger. She didn't stand a chance with those injuries. I hope we catch the prick soon before he tries to replace her."

"Crap, that's a good point. We need to do all we can to prevent this from happening again, but how?"

Dave hitched his shoulders. "You tell me. Damn, why us? Why did this land on our doorstep?"

"Look, Dave, no one in the team is going to be over the moon to be dealing with a case like this, but that should make us even more bloody determined to nail this bastard, right?"

"I agree. I still envision it being tough to sleep at night until we achieve our goal."

Kayli patted his knee. "I know. I feel the same way, and I don't even have kids. No one has the right to rob a child so young of her life. We will get this depraved individual. I guarantee it, Dave."

## 2

In a rush to get back to the station and begin the investigation, Kayli used her siren to slice through the traffic. She told Dave to return to the incident room to discuss the new case with the team while she stopped off at the Missing Persons Department on the floor below.

Barbara Wallace greeted her as soon as she stepped through the door. "Hello, stranger. How are things going?"

"Hi, Barb. I'm doing well. This isn't a social call, I'm afraid."

"Uh oh! By the look on your face, I'm sensing you've found a body you need to identify."

"Your crystal ball is working exceptionally well, as usual. I've just come from a derelict house where the body of a girl around six or seven was found. You're my first stop. There was no ID on her body, so I need to see if you have any kids who have been reported missing, let's say within the last month or so."

"Take a seat. I'll pull up the files, and we'll go through them together. Want a coffee?"

"I'd love one. White with one sugar, thanks."

Barbara flicked the switch on her computer before she headed over to the vending machine in the corner. She returned and placed a much-needed cup of coffee in front of Kayli, who sipped at the boiling-hot liquid immediately. "Right, let's see what we can find. I'll search the local area first. If nothing comes of that, I'll increase the perimeter until we locate something."

Kayli was amazed at the images filling the monitor. Barbara flipped through the files briskly, turning to face her every now and again to see if she recognised any of the children on the screen.

A full ten minutes later, Kayli shouted, "Stop! That's her. I'm sure it is."

"Jamillia Watson. She was reported missing three weeks ago."

"I don't remember seeing anything on TV about her disappearance. Why is that?"

"It was touted around. Times have changed in the media world, and the disappearance of a child isn't classed as newsworthy nowadays."

"What? I can't believe it."

"Maybe I'm being a little harsh. It was mentioned, right near the end of the bulletin I heard. They gave her a fifteen-second slot, from what I can remember."

"That's appalling. How times have changed. I suppose all this news about Brexit and the cock-ups Trump is making are far more newsworthy at the moment."

"Anyway, if this is the girl, the parents are going to be devastated to hear that their daughter is dead."

"Yeah, I can't say I'm looking forward to breaking the news to them. I think I need a couple more cups of coffee inside me before I do that. Can you print off the details for me? I take it the parents' address will be on file?"

"Definitely. I don't relish your job this afternoon. Are you going to ring them first? Make arrangements to go around to see them rather than turning up on their doorstep?"

"I think I'd rather just take the risk and show up. Either way, it's going to be an exceptionally difficult day for them after I divulge the news they've probably been dreading to hear since their daughter disappeared."

The printer churned into action, and Barbara left her chair to collect the paperwork it was spewing out. She placed it all in a pink wallet file and handed it to Kayli.

"Thanks, I really appreciate your help on this. Maybe we should search the database to see if there are any more kids who have been reported missing in the last few months in that particular area."

"I can do that and send you over a copy of the files this afternoon."

"That would be fantastic. Not sure if it will come to anything. Could be a one-off, but you know, with this type of thing, it's better to be forearmed." Kayli smiled then emptied the contents of her coffee cup and left the room. She raced up the stairs and into the incident room. Her team looked her way when she entered.

"We've got an ID on the victim," she announced. "Dave, we need to visit the parents now, before the media get wind of what's gone on at the house of horrors."

They left the station and drove the twenty-minute journey in relative silence, each of them lost in their own thoughts. "I'll tell them."

Dave turned to face her, wearing a frown. "Why say that? You always break the news to the victim's family. Why should this time be any different?"

"All right, no need to snap my head off. I was just saying. Stating the obvious I know. Ignore me then. Here it is. There's a car in the drive." Kayli inhaled and exhaled a few deep breaths before she flung open the car door and exited the vehicle.

"Good luck," Dave muttered as he rang the doorbell.

The door was opened almost immediately by a tall, handsome black man. "Yes? If you're selling double glazing, you can get lost."

Kayli produced her warrant card. "Hello. Mr. Kelvin Watson? I'm DI Kayli Bright. Can my partner and I come in and speak to you?"

His hand covered half his face. "You've found her?"

Kayli nodded curtly. "We have. Please, can we talk about this inside?"

He stepped behind the door and swept his arm in front of him, inviting them into his home. "Lorella, come quick. It's the police."

Heavy footsteps pounded floorboards in the room above, and a woman tying her dressing gown into place appeared at the top of the stairs. "Is it Jamillia? Have you found her?"

"This is my partner, DS Dave Chaplin, and we would like to talk with you. Would you care to join us and speak someplace more convenient?" Kayli asked, ignoring the woman's question.

Lorella Watson raced down the stairs, almost tripping over her dressing gown. Dave stood at the bottom of the stairs, ready to break her fall if necessary.

The woman grabbed Kayli's arm. "Please, tell me she's safe."

When Kayli didn't answer, Lorella broke down in tears and crumpled to the floor. Her husband glared at Kayli and tried to pull his wife to her feet. Lorella began screaming in between the sobs, rocking backwards and forwards, crying out her dead daughter's name. "Jamillia, baby, no!"

"I'm so sorry. Please, can we sit down and talk? I know this can't be easy."

Lorella finally accepted her husband's help to get to her feet. The couple squeezed past Kayli and Dave and entered the first door on the right in the long hallway.

Kayli found it hard to stop her nerves from showing and held her hands together in her lap as the four of them took their seats. "It is with regret that I have to inform you that a child's body was found yesterday evening."

"Are you saying that it might not be our daughter?" Mr. Watson asked.

Kayli shook her head. "The victim matched your daughter's likeness from the missing persons report you filed a few weeks ago."

Lorella and her husband stared at each other in disbelief. Moments later, Lorella broke down in tears again.

Her husband moved closer to her on the sofa and cradled her in his arms. "Hush now."

Kayli swallowed the emotions churning in her throat. "I appreciate how difficult this must be for both of you, but the more information you can give us now, the more likely it is that we'll apprehend the person who did this, and swiftly."

Kelvin nodded. "We'll tell you everything we know, which isn't much. When can we see her?"

"The post-mortem is being carried out today, and the pathologist has asked me to tell you that you can see her as soon as possible. I'll have her call you later this afternoon."

"Is she bad? Her body... what condition is it in?" Kelvin asked.

Lorella stopped crying to stare at her husband then turned to look at Kayli, her eyes wide with expectation, dreading the response.

"Her body was intact. A few broken bones. We'll know more after the pathologist has completed her examination. I'm sorry."

Lorella screamed and bolted from the room. Kelvin appeared to be in two minds whether to go after her or remain in the lounge.

"Please, go and make sure your wife is okay. We're not going anywhere for a while."

"Thank you," he mumbled before rushing out of the room.

"This is tough for them," Dave announced, rising to his feet and pacing the floor.

"We're hardly finding it a picnic, either. We need to stick with it, though. The statistics prove that most children are abducted by someone they know. We need to make them aware of that and get the ball rolling on questioning anyone connected to the little girl."

"I hear you. Do you think they'll be in the right state of mind to give us the answers? I doubt it. I know I wouldn't be after hearing that devastating news. Crap, why did she have to be dead?"

"Ssh... keep your voice down. You're obviously taking this hard. Do you want to wait in the car while I question them?"

"I'm not taking it hard—I'm bloody angry. Sorry if you'd prefer me to keep my feelings under wraps, boss."

Kayli sighed. "I'm not telling you to do that, Dave. Come on, we need to hold it together for the parents' sake. You know how these things work." Hearing footfalls on the stairs, Kayli motioned for Dave to retake his seat beside her.

Seconds later, a defeated-looking Kelvin entered the room and sat in the sofa opposite them. "She's been sick. I've put her in bed. She's under the doctor for depression, and I fear that she'll do something to herself now that she knows Jamillia isn't going to be coming back." He placed a pot of pills on the coffee table in front of him.

"I'm so sorry that your wife is struggling like this, Mr. Watson. Are you okay to answer some questions for us?"

"I'll do my best. My wife is riddled with guilt, Inspector. She was due to pick Jamillia up from school that day, but the traffic was bad, there had been an accident, and she got stuck in the hold-up. When she arrived at school, the staff told her that a friend had picked Jamillia up. Lorella tore into them. She was beside herself. No one had permission to pick up Jamillia other than my wife and myself—why would the school allow her to leave with someone else? Why have those rules in place if they're going to break them like that?"

"That's terrible. We'll definitely be seeking the answers to those questions when we go to interview the staff. In the weeks leading up to your daughter's abduction, did you notice anyone hanging around the estate?"

He fell silent for a while as he thought, then shook his head. "No, I can't recall anyone. You think this person was watching us and our routine?"

"It's not unheard of. Forgive me, but I need to ask this question because statistics in these kinds of cases often point to someone having a connection to the child, maybe a relative or a friend of the family. Does anyone come to mind?"

"What? You think a member of my family would be capable of destroying us like this? That's unthinkable, whether you're going by your damn statistics or not."

"I'm sorry. I had to ask. Do you have any male members of the family who frequently visit your home," Kayli pressed, not willing to accept him rejecting the question out of hand.

"My father and my brother, that's all. Neither of them would dream of touching my daughter inappropriately, let alone abducting her and keeping her somewhere secret for weeks. They just wouldn't. Anyway, Dad's really ill. He had a heart attack six months ago and is still recuperating. He loved Jamillia."

"You mentioned your brother. What's his name?"

"Troy, he works away from home a lot. A rep for a confectionery company. There's no way he'd hurt a hair on her head. He loved her too much, and she loved him." He scratched the side of his face. "You know what I mean. Nothing sinister in that, he just loved her. Christ, is that what this world has come to when you have to double-check what you're saying when revealing how much your family love each other? It's disgusting. As though loving a child is a terrible mistake."

"You're right, and I'm sorry for putting you through this. We're probably being over cautious, but I'd rather go down that route than put another child in harm's way. You understand our need to cover all the angles, right?"

"Sadly, yes. It doesn't make it any easier. If I give you Troy's address, how the hell is that going to look to my brother? He's going to think that I believe he had something to do with his own niece's death. Can you imagine what damage that is going to cause within our family?"

"It's tough. Obviously, we'll be discreet wherever possible if that will put your mind at ease."

"It doesn't, Inspector. How the hell has it come to this? Just over three weeks my child has been missing, and you lot haven't done a thing to try and find her."

"Have you seen your brother in that time?"

"Yes, twice. He and I even searched the streets for her together when she first went missing. Do you really expect me to believe he's capable of harming my daughter when he went out of his way to do that?"

*Most paedophiles would do the same. Keen to avoid the focus of attention landing on their doorstep.* "Maybe not. We'll still need to have a word with him. Maybe he saw something suspicious himself that he would like to share."

Kelvin left his chair and walked over to the sideboard behind him. He removed an address book and opened it, then handed the book to Kayli to jot down Troy's address.

"Has he worked as a rep on the road for long?"

"A couple of years, I suppose."

"That's really helpful. You have my word that we won't go in there all guns a-blazing."

"I'd appreciate it. Surely I would be aware if my own brother had those sick tendencies."

"That's not always the case. These people can be manipulative, not only with the children they abduct, but also with the people surrounding them in their day-to-day lives. They don't advertise the fact they 'like' children on their foreheads. If they did, it would make our lives a lot easier."

"I still think you're wrong about Troy."

"What about family friends? Anyone come to mind there?"

He shook his head. "No, all our friends have kids of their own. I refuse to believe they could be guilty of such atrocities."

"All the same, we'll need their names and addresses."

Kelvin snatched back the address book and flicked through the pages. Each time he found a relevant page, he stopped and returned the book to Kayli to jot down the names and addresses—a total of four times. "I'm begging you to do this delicately. These men have been friends of ours for years. I'd rather keep that friendship intact, if it's all the same to you."

"You have my word on that, I promise. What school did Jamillia attend?"

"Saint Agnes's Primary School. Do you need the address?"

Kayli looked at Dave. "Do you know it, Dave?"

"Yeah, on Charters Road, is that right?"

Kelvin nodded. "Yes, that's the one. It's quite a small school. They have a handful of teachers there. You don't think it could have been one of them, do you? Don't they have to be vetted or something?"

"We'll still go there and get a few statements from the teachers. They might have seen someone hanging around the school in the weeks before Jamillia was taken. Did the school say whether your daughter was picked up by a female or male?"

"I can't remember. You'll have to ask them. Everything was a blur at the time… it still is."

"Perhaps Jamillia confided in her brothers or sisters about someone hanging around. Did she have any siblings?"

"Only Marcia, she's younger than her sister, only four. She's at playgroup now. I doubt you'd get much joy out of her. I'm sure she would have told us if she knew anything."

"Okay, what about other family members, perhaps female relatives who Jamillia might have confided in?"

"I don't think so. She would have told her mother if anything was troubling her."

"Can you think of anything else we should know before we begin our investigation in earnest?"

"No, not at this moment. Can you tell me a little about your experience in such cases? I need to know that my daughter's case will be dealt with efficiently."

"Of course. I won't lie to you—this is the first case of this nature my team is dealing with, but only this morning, my DCI pulled me into her office to praise us for reaching our targets in solving cases for the year—the only team to do that at the station, I might add. Please, I can't emphasise this enough that it's very much a two-way thing. If you should think of anything you haven't mentioned during our conversation today, I need you to contact me on this number day or night. Likewise, if you or your wife need to know how the investigation is progressing, I'll do my best to keep you updated on things. Of course, it won't always be that easy if we're in the process of chasing a suspect. I just want you to know that you're in safe hands."

"Let's hope you catch the person responsible for murder... abducting my daughter before he picks up someone else's child."

"I hope that's the case, too. Can I ask what you do for a living, Mr. Watson?" His eyebrow rose as if he were surprised by the question.

"I work through the night at an all-night burger bar in Bristol. Crazy Joe's Place. Why?"

"Just filling in the blanks, sir. What about your wife. Does she work?"

"She works part-time in the shop around the corner. She was going to up her hours once Marcia was at school full-time. Not sure she'll be able to cope with that now, given what's happened."

"The name of the shop, sir?" Kayli smiled, warding off any doubts the man might have.

"It's the small Co-op in the high street. You probably passed it on your way here."

"That's great. It's just for our records. Okay, we'll get off now. I want to reassure you again that we will do everything in our power to bring the culprit to justice, hopefully soon. Ring me if you need anything."

Kelvin showed them to the front door. Kayli's heart broke in two when she heard Lorella's sobs filling the hallway from her bedroom upstairs.

"Thank you, Inspector. I better see to my wife now."

He shook first Dave's hand then Kayli's. She held on to his longer than she usually did. "Please take care of your wife. Reassure her that my team will do their best for you both."

"I will. Thank you."

## 3

Once Kayli and Dave had left the house and Kelvin Watson had closed the door behind them, they both let out a huge sigh.

"That was tough. I feel like I've been on an emotional rollercoaster," Kayli said as they exited the garden and hopped back in the car.

"Me too, and I didn't even say anything."

"Yeah, tell me something I don't know."

"What now?"

"We go back to the station and start trawling through the database. We've got a list of names to be getting on with."

"What about going to Jamillia's school?"

"I think we'll leave that until tomorrow. Let the press do their bit in reporting the murder and see if it spooks anyone overnight."

"Good thinking. I knew you were an inspector for a reason."

"Flattery will get you everywhere. I need to chase up the PM when we get back. Let's stop off and pick the team up some lunch en route."

"Generous too!" Dave chuckled.

"Did I say I was paying?"

Dave chewed on his lip, and Kayli punched him in the arm.

"I'm kidding," she said "I'll pay, this time. We need to stay focussed on this one, Dave. That woman is going to go downhill rapidly if we don't come up with a suspect soon."

"I agree. The guilt she must be feeling must be intolerable."

"Poor woman. I would hate that responsibility to be clinging to my shoulders."

They drove back to the station with only the noise of the car engine filling the inside of the vehicle. When they arrived, Kayli distributed the sandwiches, and Dave put his hand in his pocket to buy everyone a coffee. Over lunch, Kayli ran through how the meeting with the parents had gone. She ended up throwing away half her sandwich, clearly not as hungry as she thought she was.

"This one isn't going to be easy, guys. We're going to have to dig deep. Let's fight hard to give Jamillia the justice she deserves, all right?" Kayli noticed that DC Donna Travis, the youngest of the team, had barely touched her lunch, and she crossed the room to speak to her. "Donna, are you okay, love?"

When Donna glanced up, there were tears in her eyes. "Not sure, boss."

Kayli tapped her on the shoulder and ordered her to follow her to the ladies'. Once inside, the floodgates opened. Kayli tried to comfort her colleague, but Donna pulled away from her.

"All right, what am I missing here? This isn't like you, Donna. What's going on?"

Donna walked into a cubicle, tore off some toilet paper, and returned to blow her nose. "Sorry, boss. It's just me being silly, that's all."

"That's all? Donna, none of us are going to find this easy. Even I'm already feeling wrung out emotionally about this case. You need to get past this, love."

"I'm trying. It's just…"

"Just what? You can tell me."

"It's just that it's brought back some memories I thought I had successfully suppressed."

Kayli leaned against the sink and folded her arms. "What memories?" She tried to recall everything she'd read in Donna's file, but she drew a blank for anything similar to the case.

"When I was at primary school, my best friend went missing."

"I'm so sorry. I had no idea."

"I never saw her again. Her body was discovered in an old well almost four months later."

"Damn, did they find the person responsible for her murder? Was it even murder, or was it just an accident?"

"It was definitely murder, and yes they found him. It turned out to be Maggie's stepfather. Her mother felt guilty as hell once the news broke. She committed suicide the very next day. Couldn't forgive herself for inviting that man to share her home."

"That's dreadful. Had they been together long?"

"If I remember rightly, they had started dating, and he moved into the house less than six months later."

"How old were you and Maggie?"

"Seven. The thing is, I noticed a month or so before her death that Maggie had become a little distant. You know the type of thing—the smile had gone from her face, and her eyes were dead. Being only seven, I had no idea what was wrong and really didn't know how to talk to her back then. Her mother wasn't the only one who felt guilty about letting her down. I went into my shell for years. Until one day, a policeman came to our school to give us a talk on personal safety and what to do if anyone approached us in the street. My whole world changed that day. From that moment on, I knew that I wanted to join the police force. To fight the evil people walking our streets, especially those who choose children as their victims. I thought about joining Social Services but wanted to be at the sharp end, to see the bastards banged up for their crimes."

"And now? With this case? Do you think you're going to be able to handle it? There are bound to be some similarities to your friend's case, during the investigation."

"Don't worry. I'll try and put it aside. I just needed to get it out of my system, boss. I'll be even more determined to get this perp, knowing what he's done to that little girl."

Kayli launched herself off the sink and gripped Donna's arms, rubbing them. "Let me know the minute things get on top of you. Got that?"

"I'll be fine. I promise."

"Right, get rid of the snot and dry your eyes. Umm… you might need to top up your makeup before you rejoin the rest of the team." Kayli dropped her arms and stepped aside.

Donna walked up to the mirror and groaned. "Panda eyes, the bane of every woman's life. Thanks, boss. For the chat and the kick up the arse."

"Hey, no kick up the arse from me, hon. My door is always open, okay?"

"I appreciate that."

Kayli left her colleague repairing the damage to her pretty face and walked back into the incident room. The rest of the team looked her way wearing puzzled expressions. "She's fine. Right, where do we start?"

Graeme held up a bundle of files. "Barbara dropped these off while you were out, boss."

Kayli approached his desk and took the files. "Great. I asked her to gather all the information she had on children who had been reported missing in the area in the last few months. Can you handle this for me, Graeme? Note down the details and who is dealing with each individual case then give the detectives a call for me. Make them aware of the discovery of Jamillia Watson's body."

Graeme looked up from the notes he'd been jotting down. "Will do, boss."

"Perhaps you can fill us all in on what you find first thing in the morning."

He nodded his agreement, and Kayli stepped into her office to ring the pathology lab. "Naomi? It's Kayli Bright."

"Hi, Kayli, are you psychic? I was just getting around to calling you."

"Not that I know of. Have you completed the PM on Jamillia Watson?"

"I have." She exhaled a heavy breath. "Poor mite, she really went through the mill."

"Oh crap, do I need to prepare myself for what's coming next?"

"I went over a lot of it with you at the scene. In the end I discovered she had three broken ribs, a broken arm and a fractured jaw."

"That poor girl."

"That's not all. What I discovered on the inside would turn the strongest of stomachs."

"Oh, shit!"

"Let's just say the poor thing was sexually assaulted. I suspected as much at the scene but wanted to be sure before I broke the news to you."

"What? No, you're not saying this depraved individual raped her, are you?"

"That's exactly what I am saying. There was also damage to her internal organs, suggesting an object was rammed into her repeatedly."

Kayli closed her eyes and flung herself back in her chair. "What a sick shit. Can you tell if the injuries occurred before or after she died? I'm praying it's the latter."

"Sadly not. The injuries occurred whilst the little girl was alive, if anything, they probably contributed to her death."

"That's disgusting. I can't imagine what that poor child must have gone through. We visited the parents earlier. I told them that you would ring them at your earliest convenience to arrange seeing her. A word of warning, the mother is feeling terribly guilty about being late to pick her daughter up from school—caught in a traffic jam. Jamillia was missing when she finally arrived. She's on anti-depressants."

"I'm not surprised. Most parents feel some form of responsibility in instances like this. She couldn't have known what would happen to her child. I'll make sure I'm available when they arrive. As for any DNA from the suspect, there was none."

"Damn. Okay, we've got a list of people to question, and we have a list of other children who have also gone missing in the area, so hopefully, things will start to slot into place soon. While you're on the phone, can you tell me if you've dealt with any similar cases in the past few months?"

"No. This is the first child murder that has come through here this year, thankfully."

"That's a relief. Let's hope it remains that way and that we're not going to uncover something far more sinister."

"I'll second that. Right, I better be getting on. I'll call the Watsons now. By the way the time of death was within the last forty-eight hours."

"Okay and do you suspect she was taken there to be killed? I can't see anyone keeping a child in the property, can you?"

"I'm inclined to agree with you. I think she was probably being kept elsewhere for the past three weeks. I'll be in touch if I discover anything else."

"Thanks, Naomi. I appreciate that. Good luck." She hung up, bounced forward in her chair, and wandered over to the window to draw in some fresh air. *What kind of sick, evil, twisted individual could do that to an innocent little girl?*

A knock on the door disrupted her thoughts. Dave poked his head into the room. "Everything all right?"

"Not really. Come in, and I'll run through a few things with you." They both sat down and Kayli recapped what Naomi had just told her. She watched the colour drain from her partner's face, and when she thought he was going to be sick, passed the wastepaper bin over the desk to him. He set it on the floor beside him. Then she informed him of what Donna had revealed in the ladies'.

His mouth gaped open for a second or two before he found his voice. "Bloody hell! Is Donna going to be all right working this case?"

"She's going to have to be. We don't have anyone else who is a whiz on the computer like she is. We'll keep an eye on her."

"Fancy having to deal with that when you were growing up. Not surprised she wanted to join the force. I think I would have felt the same way if I'd been in her shoes."

"Me too. We just never know what's going to happen in this life and how it determines our future. Right, I think we should call it a day today. Looks like we'll have a pretty full day to contend with tomorrow. I've asked Graeme to inform us about the open cases of the other missing children in the area first thing. We'll see what comes of that before we head over to the school, okay?"

"Sounds good to me. Want me to do anything before heading off?"

"Nope, it's been an emotional day. Give Suranne and Luke a hug for me when you get home. Tell her about the case, but try not to scare her too much. I wouldn't necessarily go into detail. Your call of course, but that's how I would deal with it. She'll hear about it soon enough on the news anyway, so I'd get in first if I were you."

"I will. Might drop by the off-licence to help ease into the conversation."

"Good idea. I could do with a drink myself tonight. Goodnight, Dave."

She watched her partner walk out of the room and decided to deal with the paperwork she had pushed to one side that morning. She was still at her desk almost an hour later, long after everyone else had gone home for the evening, so she rang home. "Hi, Mark. I'm just leaving now. Want me to bring anything in with me?"

"Nope, we're all good at this end."

She noted his abrupt tone but chose to ignore it. It didn't bode well on the job front. "Okay, I'll be home in twenty. Love you."

He grunted and hung up, which was unusual for him. He never hung up without first reciprocating her endearment. She sighed, slipped on her coat, and collected her handbag before she switched off the light and left the office.

There was a commotion going on in the reception area as she walked through it. Two uniformed officers were trying to persuade a drunk to hand over the ripped carrier bag he was holding tightly against his chest. However, the drunk was adamant he wasn't going to let them have it.

"Hello, George. Remember me? What have you been up to?"

The drunk shook his head as if to clear his vision. "Ah, yes, I remember. I'd be all right if these two hoodlums would stop trying to rob me of my possessions," he slurred.

Kayli winked at the officers and held out her hand. "Hand it over, George. You'll get them back once you've slept it off in a cell."

George's mouth turned down at the sides, and he handed her the tatty carrier bag. "Only because it's you, beautiful lady."

Kayli placed the bag on the counter in front of the desk sergeant. "You need a woman's touch with these things now and again, Sergeant Donaldson."

He chuckled. "I'll bear that in mind in the future, boss. Might even give you a call to help us out on the odd occasion, if that's all right with you?"

"Sure, why not? It's not as if I have anything else to do with my time. Good evening, all."

"Hey, if you've got nothing better to do, Inspector, fancy spending the night in the cell with me?" George called out after her.

"Oh, I'll be there, George. In your dreams, love." She sniggered as she stepped out of the station into the fresh air.

Thirty minutes later, armed with a bottle of wine and four cans of beer, Kayli walked up the path to the modest terraced home she and Mark had bought two years before. She found him sitting in the lounge, watching the news. Kayli bent down to kiss him. He was glued to the screen and hadn't even noticed her arrival.

"Mark, is something wrong?" She placed the alcohol on the floor beside her and sat next to him on the couch.

"Nothing. Ssshhh… I'm watching the news. They found a child's body today in a cellar."

Kayli kicked off her shoes and tucked her legs underneath her on the chair. "I know. I'm dealing with the case. It was pretty gruesome."

"God, I'd hate to be involved in something like that. I hope you find the bastard and make him suffer. He wouldn't make it into court if I had ten minutes in a cell with him," he said, his anger evident in his words.

She reached for his hand. "Mark? What's wrong? Tell me. I know when something is up?"

"I'm sick of everything."

"Everything? Are you including *me* in that sweeping statement?"

He turned to look at her, his eyes narrowing as he shook his head. "Don't be ridiculous. You know I don't mean you. Why do you have to make out everything is always about you?"

Kayli let go of his hand, picked up the alcohol, and left the room. She didn't do arguments and would rather walk away than have a heated discussion with Mark—or anyone else for that matter. She opened the bottle of wine, poured herself a large glass then took it upstairs to run a bath. She had been soaking in the tub for a good ten minutes before a sorrowful-looking Mark eased open the door and popped his head into the bathroom.

Kayli smiled tentatively at him. "Do you want to join me?"

"Nah, I had a shower earlier. I'm sorry. You didn't deserve that."

"I can't help if you won't tell me what's wrong." The job hunting had obviously been a failure, but she needed him to tell her that.

He sat down on the toilet next to her and pulled the tab on the can of beer he was holding. "They didn't want me. I'm not sure where I go from here."

"Damn, I'm really sorry about that, love. Something is sure to turn up soon."

"Well, money is getting very tight now. If it comes down to cleaning cars or emptying the bins, then I suppose I'll have to bite the bullet and do it, but I'd rather not. I'm not sure what employers are afraid of."

"I'm at a loss to know their reasoning for rejecting you too. You'd think they would see ex-army guys as an asset. You're disciplined, hard-working, smart, not only in your choice of clothes but up here, as well." She tapped her temple.

"Maybe they class me as an unknown quantity, a killing machine, unable to function in society."

"Really? Well, they're damn stupid if they think that. It's their loss in that case, love."

"Except it's not, is it? It's my loss if no one is willing to employ me."

"We'll get through this sticky time. Dip into our savings if we have to."

"No!" he snapped.

"Whoa, okay, it was just a suggestion. I don't care about the wedding, Mark. I'd rather have you not walking around here with a long face."

He stared at her for a while. "I'm sorry if I'm such a grouch. Maybe I'll take my beer and leave you alone if that's how you feel." He left the room and slammed the door behind him, making her flinch.

*Crap! Well done for making things a thousand times worse.*

Not long after, she heard the front door slam also. "Award yourself a gold star for ballsing that up, girlie." She continued to soak in the bath for a few minutes then got out, towelled herself dry, and pulled on her dressing gown. She debated whether to get dressed again, to go out and search for Mark, but whenever he'd stormed off in a huff before, she had been unable to find him. *None of this would be happening if only someone would show faith in him and give him a job.*

Then, as if a lightbulb switched on in her head, an idea struck her. He could apply to the force for a job. They had recruited several ex-servicemen and women in the past. She intended to run it past him when he returned... *if* he returned.

Kayli knocked up a cheese omelette for herself and switched on Sky News, the only programme she knew would repeat their news bulletins constantly, hoping to catch what they had divulged to the public regarding Jamillia's case. The little girl's wide smile filled the screen. Sudden tears moistened Kayli's eyes, and she brushed them away with the back of her hand. "Such a sweet, innocent-looking little girl. How could anyone even contemplate raising their hand to her, let alone...?"

Kayli must have fallen asleep on the sofa because the next thing she knew, she felt Mark's arms around her, and he was carrying her upstairs to bed.

"You came back," she said breathlessly.

He smiled. The creases of anger around his eyes had been replaced by loving crinkles. "Of course, I did. It would take a lot to get rid of me, you know that. I'm sorry, sweetheart."

They reached the bedroom, where he placed her gently on the bed. She pulled him down on top of her and kissed him. Everything would be all right between them—she was positive about that.

# 4

Kayli and Mark were still cuddling each other when the alarm went off the next morning at seven o'clock. "Argh... I need to get a move on. We have a lot to do and lots of people to interview." She kissed his neck and flung back the quilt.

Fifteen minutes later, she was in the spare room, drying her hair with one hand and trying to fasten her blouse with the other. Mark had gone back to sleep and was snoring quietly.

Eager to begin her day, she left the house without eating breakfast and drove into work. Aware that the rush-hour traffic would be thickening within the next few minutes, she put her foot down, in hopes of avoiding it. Kayli smiled when she saw Donna parking her vehicle in the car park when she pulled in. "Hi, Donna. How are you feeling about things today?"

"I'm good. I gave myself a stern talking-to last night—crikey, that sounds bad. I don't often talk to myself, I promise."

Kayli chuckled. "I believe you. Glad you're okay today and ready to jump in. I have a feeling we're going to need your expertise on the computer for this case."

"How come?"

Kayli sighed. "Let's see what the morning meeting churns out first, and then I'll share with the team what my thinking is about this case and what we could be dealing with."

"I think I can guess. A paedophile ring, right?"

"You're smart. I'm extremely fortunate to have you on my team. That is indeed what I'm thinking. I fear this investigation is going to be one of the toughest we've ever had to handle, but in the end, once we've caught the person—or persons—involved, it will also prove to be our most satisfying. And mark my words, I'll not rest easy until we arrest every fucker involved."

"I came to the same conclusion, boss. There are just too many of these cases cropping up in the news these days; it was only a matter of time before one surfaced on our patch."

"You're spot on there. Let's not be too hasty. We'll see what Graeme has to tell us first about the research I gave him to deal with yesterday, and then go from there. Look, if during the investigation you need time out, please don't hesitate to give me the nod or feel free to take me to one side, all right?"

"I promise. Thanks for being so understanding, boss. I'm sure I'll be okay. A good cry usually puts things into perspective for me."

"Maybe I should give that a try now and again." Kayli laughed as they entered the station together. She could have cried last night when the love of her life walked out on her for hours, but she'd refused to do that. That wasn't to say Mark's actions hadn't hurt her, but she hadn't wanted him to come home and find her a snivelling wreck. She preferred to bury her feelings when something upset her. She saw it as keeping Mark on his toes when she hid her true feelings from him. If she'd learnt one thing from her mother over the years, that was to never lay all her cards on the table where men were concerned.

Thinking of Mark reminded her that she hadn't covered the subject about him joining the force, so she decided to give him a call on the way up the stairs.

"Yep."

She cringed, hearing his groggy voice. "Hi, love. Sorry, did I wake you?"

"No. I was just about to jump in the shower. What have you forgotten?"

She stopped walking and watched Donna enter the incident room. She leaned against the wall to continue her conversation. "I was thinking while you were out last night. Why don't you apply for a job with the police? I could pick up an application form for you today, if you like."

"What? Are you crazy? I'd kill half the offenders. I ain't got the patience to deal with people like that. I'll find something soon... I better, otherwise, you're likely to dump me."

"Thanks for having such a low opinion of me. Okay, it was worth a shot. Gotta fly now. See you later. Hope you have a productive day."

"Job hunting, you mean? Yeah, I'll be out there, pounding the streets," he said, sounding peeved. "Don't worry your pretty head about that."

Kayli ended the call and sighed. *Oh well, that's the last I'm going to say on the subject.* She pushed open the door to find the team looking in her direction. She frowned. "Something wrong?"

Donna held up a pile of messages. Kayli walked across the room and took them from her hand. Flicking through them, she could understand her team's reaction. "Good to see the media coverage has sparked some interest, although I'm not liking where some of these messages have come from. Graeme, do you recognise any of these names?"

"Yes, boss."

"Okay, I suggest we all grab a coffee and listen to what Graeme has to say first, then we'll deal with the messages."

Dave leapt out of his seat and headed towards the vending machine. Donna joined him while Kayli slipped into her office to see what paperwork awaited her. Thankfully, there wasn't a lot. She wanted to press on with the case at full steam, without the hindrance of dealing with nonsensical triteness from head office.

When she returned to the outer office, Dave had handed out all the drinks and everyone had assembled in front of the whiteboard. Graeme was standing alongside it with his notes in his hand.

"Do you want me to fill in the board while you go through your research, Graeme?" Kayli suggested.

"That would be a great help, boss. Thanks."

"Let me have a slurp of coffee first, then begin in your own time." She gulped down a few mouthfuls of the hot, strong liquid and felt it slip past her throat.

"I'm ready when you are."

She nodded. "Okay, everyone, Graeme has put a lot of hard work into this, so listen up, and as we have a lot to get through, please don't interrupt. We'll deal with any questions afterwards. Take it away, Graeme."

He cleared his throat then studied his notes for a few seconds before he began. "Obviously, we have our first victim, Jamillia Watson. The Missing Persons Department issued us with the files of three other local kids who have been reported missing in the past few months. I spoke to a few of the detectives dealing with those investigations, and they all told me pretty much the same—that clues had dried up and they were left flummoxed. I asked the detectives involved why they hadn't connected the cases, and they all said they had thought about it, but as all three disappeared under different circumstances, they felt it would be better to treat them as individual cases."

Kayli chewed the inside of her mouth. "Not something I would have done myself, but I suppose we're looking at it from another angle because we have a body."

"I was thinking along those lines too, boss."

"Carry on, Graeme. I'll try to keep my mouth zipped from now on." She shrugged and smiled.

"First up is Victoria Smalling, an eight-year-old white girl. She's been missing the longest, nearly four months. She went to a swing park with her friends and went missing on her walk home. She's also the furthest in our search area. Her parents live in Weston-Super-Mare. When I spoke to the detective dealing with the case, he said that the parents had pretty much given up any hope of seeing their child again."

"That's so sad, but understandable. I think I would always have hope as long as my child's body hadn't been recovered."

"I agree, boss."

Donna raised her hand to speak. "I remember seeing the name Smalling in the messages I handed you, boss."

Kayli looked through the messages and set one aside. "You did indeed. Okay, I'll ring the parents in a bit."

Graeme nodded then continued, "Next up is Lucy Dolan, a seven-year-old white girl, talented ballet dancer at her local dance school. Disappeared on her way to the shops when she was running an errand for her mother in the Temple Meads area of the city. Busy area, not sure I'd let a daughter of that age out on her own. The dad is a taxi driver, and he's had his colleagues out there searching for her but received negative results. She's been gone six weeks now."

Kayli jotted a reminder in her notebook to look up the dance school.

"The final girl is Sonia Fisher. White and eight-years-old. She disappeared four weeks ago from the primary school playground, during the day. Should never happen, in my book. Apparently, the parents have split up over the incident, each blaming the other, which is daft really, when it was out of their hands. The school is to blame. This might flag up something, boss. The primary school is a few streets away from the school Jamillia attended."

Kayli finished writing down the information on the board and added Jamillia Watson's name and the facts they knew about her disappearance. "So, what can we glean from this?" She circled the time each child had disappeared. "Apart from Victoria Smalling, all the other girls went missing a few weeks apart from each other. Why the gap between Victoria Smalling and the others?"

"Maybe there's no connection to the other three," Dave suggested.

"I'm thinking along the lines that perhaps the offenders abducted her first then panicked before they risked taking another child, and now that they've taken three more, they've found it easy to abduct and are holding the kids somewhere."

"Could be. You think they'll strike again then?"

Kayli nodded. "Definitely, unless airing Jamillia's death via the media has sent them into a frenzy. Only time will tell. I just hope they don't panic, kill the kids and move on, or worse still, if they are holding all the kids somewhere together that they pack up and leave the kids to fend for themselves." Kayli shuddered at the thought.

"There again, the media attention might make them more daring. They could attempt to abduct yet more children," Graeme added.

"That's always a possibility. You know how much some criminals enjoy giving us the runaround and poking fun at us." She rubbed her cheek as she thought. "Another thing is puzzling me. Three of the children are white, and Jamillia was black. Is there any significance in that? Also, why is Jamillia's body the only one to be recovered, and yet she was the last girl to disappear? If these abductions are all connected, something isn't adding up. Going forward, I'm in two minds whether to treat the cases as linked. What do you guys think?"

Dave shrugged. "What harm can it do linking the cases? It's better to do that from the outset, in my mind."

Kayli nodded. "Donna? What do you think we should do?"

Donna tilted her head from side to side as she contemplated the question. "I think I have to agree, boss. Treat them as if they're linked."

"Graeme?"

He nodded. "I have to agree. What do we have to lose?"

"That's agreed then. Right, I'll go through the messages in my office and see which ones we should either ditch or chase up."

"Thinking about it, boss, I seem to recall the mother of one of the other girls contacted us also," Donna pointed out.

"I'll set that one aside and contact the two sets of parents myself. For now, we need to do all we can with the Watson case. Donna, can you do a background check on Lorella and Kelvin Watson. Also, a Troy Watson, who is Kelvin's brother, plus… hang on…" She flipped through her notebook, found the page she was looking for, and handed it to Donna. "These are the names of four male friends of Kelvin's. Check them out too while you're at it."

"On it now, boss."

"Dave, you can help me sift through these, and, Graeme, you said you hadn't managed to contact all the detectives working the other cases as yet. Can you try and put that right this morning?"

"Will do, boss."

Kayli picked up her cup of lukewarm coffee and the messages then walked through to her office. She set half the messages down on one side of the desk for Dave to sift through while she tackled the other half. She placed the messages from the Smallings and the Dolans on the priority pile. Ten minutes later, she and Dave had whittled the piles down to five messages of significance.

"What do you want to do next? I thought we were going out to the school first thing."

Kayli nodded. "That's still my intention. I think the parents will be anxiously waiting for my call, however. I'll ring them first, and then we'll go. How's that?"

He rose from his chair. "Fine by me. Just give me a shout when you're done."

Kayli inhaled a large breath before she dialled the first number. The call was answered almost immediately. "Hello, is that Mrs. Smalling?"

"It is."

"Hi, I'm returning your call from last night. I'm DI Kayli Bright."

"Does this mean you're taking over my daughter's case? Someone needs to—we've been left in the dark for months now. That can't be right, can it? Someone has my child, Inspector, and I really can't stand being left in the dark anymore. I've had to deal with the longest four months of my life. If she's dead, then I want to be able to grieve and move on. I'm sorry if that sounds harsh to you, but being in a state of limbo for as long as we have is putting a terrible strain on our health and our marriage."

"I'm sorry for everything you've been through. My team and I are dealing with a murder enquiry, the one aired on TV last night. At this stage, I can understand how put out you must be with the officers dealing with your case, but there really isn't any more I can tell you about Victoria's disappearance. Please, will you give me a little time to discuss the case with the officer dealing with it? Then I'll get back to you."

"That seems to be the only thing you officers do well—'discuss the case'. But what we need is people out there searching for our little girl."

Kayli could hear the woman's voice faltering as the emotions welled up. "Please, you have my assurance that we'll do all we can to find your daughter and to bring her home to you."

"Words are cheap, Inspector. What we need is action. I know we're just normal working-class people. Is it only the likes of that doctor couple—the McCanns, who are allowed to have the funds of the state flung at them to help find their daughter? Yes, I'm angry. Why should people have to listen to the media going on about *one* child in particular? That case has been given more air time than the election. Yet our daughter has only ever been mentioned once, and that was in the form of a small sentence aired on the local news, not even the national news. Doesn't every mother deserve the right to be treated the same way?"

"I'm with you one hundred percent on that, Mandy. Is it all right if I call you Mandy?"

"Of course, it is. I'm glad someone appears to be taking our case seriously. My child went missing after spending time with her friends. I didn't go out to dinner and leave her alone in an apartment, so why haven't I been given the same rights as those two doctors? I'm sorry, but as you can see, I'm very angry about this. I've tried to get my voice heard, but their case always takes priority. It's frustrating as hell to hear that over ten million pounds have been spent trying to find that one child, and to crown it all, the child didn't even go missing in this country. What the fuck is that all about? Excuse my language."

"Seriously, I totally agree with you, but I've only just learned about your case. Please bear with me for a few days, as I'm hoping the information we gather from the other cases we're working on will, in turn, have a major impact on your case."

"Let's hope so. I'm begging you not to treat Victoria as just another statistic, Inspector. Our daughter means the absolute world to us. She's our only child, and we're desperate to have her back… if she's still alive that is. We've all but given up hope of ever seeing her again. I apologise for tearing you off a strip. I understand it's not your fault, but

I'm at my wits' end. Not knowing whether she's dead or alive is destroying us, Inspector."

"I know, and I promise to get back to you in the next day or two. Please understand that I have no intention of pushing your case aside."

"I believe you. I don't have any option not to believe you. Please bring Victoria back to me soon." The woman's bubbling anger finally subsided.

"My team and I will do our very best. I'll be in touch soon." Kayli reeled off her phone number to the woman then hung up. She inhaled and exhaled numerous times to calm her racing heart then dialled the Dolans' number.

On the fourth ring, a weary-sounding female answered, "Hello?"

"Mrs. Dolan?"

"Yes, if this is some kind of survey, I'm not in the mood to deal with you today. Goodbye."

"It's not. Please don't hang up, Katrina. I'm DI Kayli Bright from the Avon and Somerset Constabulary. I'm following up on your call to the station last night. Do you have time for a quick chat?"

"I have all the time in the world. I sit all day, just looking out my front window, waiting for my baby to come home. Where is she, Inspector?"

"My team have only just been made aware of your daughter's disappearance. All I'm doing at this stage is touching base with you to assure you that we're going to be working alongside the original officers on the case. We're investigating a murder that we suspect is linked to Lucy's disappearance."

"Murder? Does that mean you think she's dead?"

"No, not at this time. The fact that your daughter and three other girls were abducted within a thirty-mile radius makes us think that the cases could be linked. We might be proved wrong about that further down the line, but it's a risk we're willing to take for now."

"Thank God. The detective dealing with the case so far has been worse than useless. I've complained a number of times that he refuses to keep me informed, but my complaints have always fallen on deaf ears. I'm thankful that my daughter's case will be looked at with fresh eyes."

"I hope my team and I don't let you down. All I ask is that you'll be patient with us, if that's okay? We're hoping that the murder enquiry will lead us to the person or persons who abducted Lucy. I don't suppose you've had any contact with anyone? Someone seeking a reward, perhaps?" Kayli kicked herself for not asking Mrs. Smalling the same question. However, Mrs. Smalling's frustrations regarding a high-profile case that had never sat well with Kayli—or any of her colleagues, in fact—had steered that conversation off course.

"No, nothing. We would have re-mortgaged the house if the bastards had contacted us. I just want my daughter back. You can understand that, can't you?"

"I can. Okay. At least we know money isn't the motive here."

"Does that matter?"

Kayli bit down on her lip, aware that her mouth had run away with her. She shouldn't have said that. "It's just one thing to cross off our list, that's all. Okay, I'll be in touch within a day or two. I'm going to give you my direct number. Do you have a pen and paper handy?"

"Yes, go ahead."

Kayli gave the woman her phone number. "Ring me if you think of anything else that could help regarding Lucy."

"I will. Please, don't lie to me, Inspector. All we need is to be kept in the loop. We have that right, yes?"

"Of course, and I'll do my very best to do that. Take care." Kayli ended the call, feeling desperately sorry for the parents she'd spoken to.

Sighing, she looked through the other messages and rang another four people who had reported witnessing something odd—and that included seeing a strange van lingering around places where kids usually played. She arranged for uniformed police to drop by during the day to take down a statement from each of them.

Kayli looked at her watch. It was almost eleven thirty. Dave had popped into the office now and again to top up her coffee. Apart from that, he'd kept his distance, until she looked up and saw him standing in the doorway, fidgeting.

"Something wrong?" she asked.

"I thought you said you wanted to take a trip out to the school this morning."

"I know. Time just passed me by. Hey, it's not as if I've been sat on my arse doing bugger all, mate. What time do schools break up for lunch? Any idea?"

"Negative. Used to be around twelve when I was at school, as far as I can remember."

"It'll probably be better to go during the lunch hour. Turning up at that time might piss the head and the teachers off, but that's tough. We need to interview everyone on the premises who were there when Jamillia went missing."

"Good thinking. Want to set off now then?"

"Why not? You can fill me in on what the team have been up to during the morning on the way."

Dave nodded and left the room.

Kayli decided she had time to make one final call, to her brother. "Hello, Giles." He was thirty-four, her senior by four years.

"Sis? What's up? Unusual for you to ring me during the day."

"Just a quickie as I have to go out. Have you spoken to Mark lately?"

"Not for a few weeks. Why?"

Kayli sighed heavily. "I'm worried about him. I thought you could either take him out for a pint or drop round to see him. I think he could do with a manly chat with someone right now. Any chance?"

"Of course. How about this evening? Still no good on the job front I take it?"

"Would you? That would be great. No news yet. It's getting him down now. Listen, he'd do his nut if he thought I was playing nurse-maid to him."

"You can count on me to be discreet. Don't worry about that. Any chance of some tea if I drop round this evening?"

She laughed. "I knew there would be a catch. Okay, it'll just be a makeshift meal, though. There's no telling what time I'll get home this evening, as it depends how things go during the day. I'm working on that child murder case that is all over the news. Thankfully, I've managed to keep out of the media's way up until now."

"Damn, I saw that. Must be a terrible case to work. Don't envy you there. I'll drop round about six then, while Annabelle is bathing Bobby. See you later."

"Bye for now, hon. Just make sure you come up with a reasonable excuse for dropping round unexpected."

"You worry too much. Leave it with me. Bye for now."

Kayli hung up and left the office in search of her partner, who was leaning against the desk by the door and jumped to his feet when she walked towards him. "Holding you up, was I, Dave?"

"Just eager to get over there, boss."

"Me too. Let's go."

Kayli drove as Dave filled her in on what Donna had found out about Jamillia's parents. "Nothing much to be honest, boss. Clean as a nun's panties. I left Donna dissecting the uncle's background."

"I think we're barking up the wrong tree looking at the family if Jamillia's murder is linked to the other three missing girls. However, it's better to cover our backs. I've arranged for uniform to take statements from the four people who rang in to report suspicious behaviour near schools and play areas. I also rang Mrs. Smalling and Mrs. Dolan to assure them that we're doing everything we can to find their daughters."

"I bet they're pissed off about how the investigations have progressed so far."

"You could say that. Who could blame them?"

"I guess. But you know as well as I do, it's hard to track these kids down if someone is intent on hiding them... if they're not dead by now. If those two kids hadn't stumbled into that building a couple of days ago, who knows how long Jamillia's body would have remained there undiscovered."

"You're right... Maybe we should get uniform to check every derelict building in Bristol."

"Christ, that would take them years. I could get a team to check the other wrecks in that row, though."

"Yep, can you sort that out for me, Dave? Let's hope we get somewhere with the school. I think we're in for an interesting few hours."

"You reckon?" Dave replied, his words laced with sarcasm.

## 5

*A*s they pulled up outside the school, kids erupted into the playground, joyful to be let loose from the confines of their classrooms.

"We couldn't have timed that any better if we'd tried," Kayli said, switching off the engine after parking the car in the school's car park.

"Screaming kids. It's like being at home," he joked, light-heartedly.

"Oops! Hey, you're the one who wanted the child, I seem to remember."

"Actually, it was a joint decision. I love Luke to bits, but sometimes wish that we could have rented a baby for a week to know what we were letting ourselves in for. I guess all parents think that, don't they?"

She laughed as she exited the car. "Probably. Crikey, Luke's only sixteen months old. He's not likely to get up to much at that age, is he?"

"You'd be surprised." He laughed. "I caught the little tyke having a swig out of my beer the other day... well, let's say he tried. Suranne prevented him from lifting the can to his mouth. She had a right go at me as if it were my fault."

"Oh dear. You'll need to be more vigilant. I hear you have to have eyes in the back as well as the front when they start crawling. It's even worse when they reach puberty."

"It's certainly been an eye-opener so far. Wouldn't change it for the world, though. He has us in fits of laughter most of the time."

After Kayli and Dave had identified themselves through the intercom system, the door buzzed open. They walked through the main entrance of the school and into a long narrow corridor, where the walls were covered with crayon drawings the kids had obviously created.

Dave stopped to study a group of pictures and whispered, "Do you think some of these children are aliens?"

"Huh? How do you make that out?"

He puffed out his cheeks and looked at her. "Because some of these pictures are out of this world."

Kayli dug him in the ribs and sniggered. "Wise arse. I wouldn't let the head hear you speaking so disparagingly about his or her pupils' masterpieces, matey."

"Seriously though, how can you make out some of these... er pictures?"

"Leave it, Dave. It's not worth using your brain power to figure out one of life's mysteries, I promise you."

They continued on their journey to the end of the hallway, where a door was labelled Reception. Kayli pushed open the door to find two secretaries tapping away on their computers.

The older of the two ladies smiled and approached the counter. "Hello there. What can I do for you?"

Kayli flashed her warrant card. "Hi, thanks for letting us in. Is it possible to have a word with the headmaster or mistress please?"

"I don't see why not. I'll check if Mrs. Laughlin has time to see you." The chubby woman bustled out of the office and returned a few moments later. She raised a flap in the counter and invited them to follow her through to another office.

A grey-haired, bespectacled lady welcomed them with an outstretched hand. "Hello, I'm the headmistress here, Mrs. Laughlin. I presume this is about Jamillia Watson?"

*The Missing Children*

"Hi, I'm DI Kayli Bright, and this is my partner, DS Dave Chaplin."

Dave shook hands with the headmistress. "Pleased to meet you."

"We're the investigating officers dealing with Jamillia's tragic case. Do you have ten minutes for a chat?"

"Of course. Please, take a seat." Mrs. Laughlin slid behind her desk, and Kayli and Dave sat down opposite her.

Dave took out his notebook, ready to jot down any significant information.

"Such a terrible situation, and the outcome was totally unexpected," Mrs. Laughlin said. "I hope the poor child didn't suffer too much before her death."

"Unfortunately, she did suffer. However, I'd rather not go into details about that."

Her hand swept over her face, and the colour drained from her cheeks. "Oh my… that poor child. She was such an adorable little girl. I can't begin to tell you how sorry I am that she was taken from the premises. I've barely slept a wink since the incident occurred."

"Maybe you can tell us how she was taken? I thought schools had safety procedures in place to prevent this type of thing from happening."

"We do. Usually, those procedures are tight and work really well, but this was one of those times when procedures let one of our pupils down. The children were out in the playground with one of the teachers and one of our teaching assistants, awaiting the parents to pick them up. The teacher had to deal with an incident—one of the children had fallen over and grazed his knee. She brought him inside to bathe the wound and patched him up with a plaster, and when she returned she found the young teaching assistant going frantic in the school playground."

"Did the assistant see who took Jamillia?"

"Yes, a young woman dropped by, said Jamillia had to go home quickly because her mother had been injured in some kind of accident. It wasn't until the assistant saw the van drive away at speed that something clicked and she realised she'd made a dreadful mistake."

"I see. Is the teaching assistant around now?"

"She only came back to work this week. She's been distraught since Jamillia went missing. I told her to take a few weeks off to get her head straight. She's been in the staffroom this morning, sobbing her heart out. I tried to persuade her to go home, but she wouldn't hear of it. Naturally, the guilt is weighing heavily on her shoulders, and there isn't a thing anyone can say or do to make her feel any better."

Kayli could understand the assistant feeling guilty, but as far as sympathy went, she couldn't bring herself to feel sorry for the young woman who'd failed so miserably in her responsibility to care for Jamillia. "Do you think she'll be up to speaking to us?"

"Only if you tread carefully, Inspector. I fear that any more pressure from the police might send her over the edge. I'd hate to have her death on my conscious, as well as little Jamillia's. I would like to help in any way we can, going forward with the case."

"We'd like to question your staff. If that's okay. Did Jamillia have one main teacher, or was she taught by all the teachers in some kind of rotation? I don't have children, so I'm unfamiliar with the workings of modern-day schooling. I'm sure things have changed drastically since I was at school."

"She had one main teacher, Mr. John Briggs."

"Is he at work today?"

"Yes. Would you like me to send for him?"

"Perhaps we can conduct the interviews in a quiet corner in the staffroom, if there is one."

"Of course. Do you want to start now?"

Kayli nodded. "The sooner, the better. Will your staff mind their lunch being interrupted?"

"I hope not. This is important, after all. I'll show you through to the staffroom."

The three of them left the office, followed the corridor past the main entrance, and veered off to the right at the end. The staffroom was smaller than Kayli had anticipated, and she glanced around the room at the six people eyeing them with interest. She tapped Mrs.

Laughlin on the arm and asked in a hushed voice, "Maybe we can interview them in a classroom instead?"

"Very well. Will next door do?"

"Perfect." The only man in the room caught Kayli's eye. He was tall, slim and around forty. He paused as he filled his cup with coffee granules, smiled at Kayli before returning to complete his task.

"Can I have your attention please?" Mrs. Laughlin addressed her staff. "These are DI Bright and DS Chaplin. They're here to interview you all about Jamillia Watson. I expect you to give them your full cooperation. We all want the suspect who snatched Jamillia caught, don't we? Well, the police can't do that without our valuable help." She pointed at the youngest person in the room. "Samantha, why don't you go first?"

The startled young blonde stared at the headmistress in disbelief. "Me? Why me?"

"Come now, that's obvious... at least it should be. Time is wasting. Off you go with the detectives." Mrs. Laughlin beckoned her with her hand and a reassuring smile. "I'm sure there's nothing for you to worry about." Mrs. Laughlin pointed to the right. "First door in the hallway, Inspector. There shouldn't be anyone in there. Samantha will be with you in a moment. I'll just have a quiet word with her first. Then I'll send the next person in once you've finished interviewing her."

Kayli and Dave left the room and waited patiently next door for Samantha to join them. Nearly five minutes later, Samantha appeared in the doorway, fresh tears in her eyes and mascara staining her cheeks.

"Do you need a moment to compose yourself? I want to assure you that you're not in any trouble, Samantha. We're simply here to gather all the facts of what happened that day."

"I know. I'm sorry. I'm just so upset by it all still. It's hard to handle when something horrendous like this happens when you're supposed to be watching out for the children. I've barely closed my eyes for weeks now, and when I do drift off, all I see is Jamillia crying out for help. Seeing the news last night... you know, that Jamillia's body... had been found, murdered..." She pulled a tissue from her sleeve as the sobs overwhelmed her again.

Kayli left her seat, slung her arm around Samantha's shoulders, and guided her to the chair. "Take your time. Can you tell us how the incident occurred?"

"Yes, Mrs. Callard had to deal with one of the children who had injured himself in the playground. She's our designated first-aid expert at the school, although there are plans to ensure we all attend a course in the near future."

"I see. Then what?" Kayli asked, aware of the young woman's nervous waffling.

"I was outside, waiting for the parents to show up to collect their children, when this young white woman came up to me and said that Jamillia's mother had been injured and had sent her to collect her daughter. She sounded genuine enough, and Jamillia recognised her. I know I shouldn't have let her take Jamillia, and I've regretted my actions every day since, I swear. It wasn't until I saw this woman bundle Jamillia into the waiting van and speed off that I realised what had happened. I ushered the other children into the school and ran to tell the head immediately. I was devastated—still am. Knowing that I've caused that little girl to lose her life is something that will crucify me for the rest of my life."

"It's hard to give you words of sympathy when I know it would be pointless. You need to accept that there are dangerous people out there and the school has put certain rules in place to ensure that this type of thing doesn't happen. I don't think anyone blames you personally for this, Samantha. If they had, you would have lost your job there and then."

"I know, and Mrs. Laughlin has been so kind, giving me a couple of weeks off, but when I returned and learned that Jamillia had died... well, everything came flooding back—the memory of that day and the guilt I've felt in the past few weeks. I'm just beside myself. I can't stop crying. I feel so responsible and keep going over and over the what-ifs in my head. Do you think it will be all right with the parents if I attend her funeral? I'm desperate to pay my respects but fear they will have a go at me."

Kayli chewed her lip. "If I were in your shoes, I'd give the funeral a wide berth. Let the family grieve in peace. It might agitate them if you turn up for the service. Perhaps light a candle at home or here at the school and hold your own vigil for her." Kayli hadn't a clue where that idea had come from, but it sounded a plausible alternative even to her ears.

"I'll do that, thank you."

"A few more questions, and then we're done. Did you notice any signwriting on the van or happen to see any of its registration number?"

"No, it was too fast for me to see, and it weaved between the parked cars, so the plate was hidden most of the time. The van was plain white. I know that's not very helpful, sorry."

"It's fine. Would you recognise the woman again? I know it's been a few weeks."

"I think I'd recognise her, but I'm not sure. I told the policeman dealing with the case back then the same thing, but nothing came of it."

"That's strange. Would you be willing to work with a police sketch artist now, or is it too late?"

"I could try. I'm willing to do anything to help you find the abductors."

"In the weeks leading up to the abduction, did you notice any strange vehicles in the area? The van perhaps?"

"I don't think so. It was quite a long time ago now, sorry."

"Never mind. Okay, if I send an artist around to see you, would you prefer that was at school or at home?"

"Either, I'm easy. Maybe it would be better at home. Mrs. Laughlin has been so understanding about things up until now, but I'd hate to overstep the mark. Saying that, my home is a tip, a one-room bedsit in the attic of a house. That's all I can afford around here on my wages. Teaching assistants are only paid just above the minimum wage, you see."

"I'll run it past Mrs. Laughlin before we leave then. Thanks for your time, and try not to beat yourself up about this too much. I know that's going to be difficult, but try."

"I will. Thank you. I hope you find that woman and her accomplice quickly before they try and take another child."

"So do we. Can you ask Mrs. Laughlin to send Mr. Briggs in next, please? Oh, and here's my card. Ring me day or night if you remember anything that you think we should know." Kayli handed her a business card and watched her leave the room. Once Samantha was on the other side of the door, Kayli turned to Dave and said, "Crap, I really would hate to be in her shoes. Poor girl must be going through hell. I didn't think I'd have much sympathy for her, but my heart went out to her in the end."

"Yeah, but then, it was her responsibility to keep an eye on the kids."

"You're all heart, Davey boy."

The door opened before Dave could respond. The tall man Kayli had locked gazes with in the staffroom entered and approached them.

"I'm John Briggs, Jamillia's teacher." He extended his hand.

Kayli slipped her hand into his. "Ah, yes. Any help you can give this investigation will mean that we can track down the suspects before they kill another child."

"I realise that, Inspector. I know how these investigations pan out," he said abruptly.

*Another one who sits at home watching the True Crime channel. Suddenly, everyone is an expert in police procedures.*

"Then perhaps you can tell us what type of child Jamillia was at school?"

"She was a very happy child, most of the time, very willing to learn. I would actually put her in the top two in the class for aptitude," his tone softened as he spoke about the child.

"You said 'most of the time'. Care to enlighten us on what you mean by that?"

"Every child has good days and bad days during their time at school."

"Are you saying there were some bad days just before she went missing?"

"Yes and no. I'm not one to cast aspersions, Inspector, but sometimes, Jamillia arrived at school in a quiet mood, which usually dissipated during the morning lessons. She loved being at school, interacting with her fellow pupils."

"Not wishing to cast aspersions, but in saying that, you're hinting that things weren't well at home for the little girl, Am I right?"

"Possibly. Maybe you should ask her parents that," he said, fidgeting in his seat.

"Oh, I will, but first, I want to know if Jamillia ever suggested there was anything wrong at home."

"She used to say the odd thing now and again." He looked down at his clenched hands on the desk in front of him.

"Come on, Mr. Briggs. I feel you're deliberately being evasive. Be open with us... unless you'd rather conduct this interview down at the station."

He sighed. "She told me once that her father had touched her inappropriately."

Kayli turned sharply to look at her partner, whose eyes were as round as footballs. Turning back to Briggs, she asked, "Did you report this conversation to Mrs. Laughlin?"

"No."

"May I ask why?"

"I was in an awkward situation. The child confided in me and also told me not to tell anyone else."

"Doesn't this school have some sort of school rule that if a child confides in her teacher, that conversation should be noted down in the school's records, shouldn't it?"

He kept quiet for the longest pause. "I'm at fault there. This is the first incident of its kind that I've come across. I was put in an impossible position."

"Have you made the head aware of this conversation since Jamillia's disappearance?"

"No. It's been torture knowing that I could have saved that little girl when she reached out to me for help."

"Yes, I can understand that and really think it was your responsibility to speak out about this. Isn't that what teachers are supposed to do? Shield the children in their care from the dangers in this life? Or am I overstating things there?"

"You can't make me feel any guiltier, I assure you. If I could turn back the clock, I would do it in a heartbeat. It's not me you should be angry with, Inspector—it's Jamillia's father who touched her inappropriately."

"I wasn't aware that I was showing any anger, Mr. Briggs. I apologise if you feel that was how it was coming across. I'm just baffled that you let this situation fester instead of doing all you could to put a stop to it."

He remained silent, wringing his hands together as he thought.

"Mr. Briggs?" Kayli prompted.

He shrugged. "What more do you want me to say? I've told you what occurred, and yet you're making out all this is my fault."

"I apologise, as that was not my intention. All I'm trying to ascertain is why a person in your authority would neglect to tell someone if a sexual abuse case was presented to them. Surely, the investigating officer should have been made aware of this when the child went missing, right?"

"I don't know. Yes, maybe I'm at fault. I'm sorry. It won't happen again. The second a child utters anything along those lines again, I will go straight to Mrs. Laughlin's office to inform her."

"What did Jamillia actually tell you?"

"Just that her father had touched her somewhere he shouldn't have."

"I see. If a child said that to me, I would have mentioned it to my superior immediately. Never mind, setting that debacle aside for the time being, leading up to Jamillia's abduction, did you see anyone hanging around the school who shouldn't have been here?"

"Not that I can recall. It was a few weeks ago, though."

"Anything at all? A person, persons, or a white van?"

"No, nothing is coming to mind."

"How long have you been a teacher at this school, Mr. Briggs?"

He lifted his head, and their eyes met. "I don't see what that has to do with anything, Inspector."

"Humour me," she snapped back.

"I've worked here for five years."

"And before that?"

"I was working as a private tutor. I really don't see what this has to do with anything."

"We're just trying to obtain as much background information about the witnesses as we can. We're not singling you out for any reason other than that you likely knew Jamillia better than the other teachers. I promise you that."

"Glad to hear it. I've never had a blemish on my career in the past and would appreciate it if that remained the case going forward, Inspector. I hope you're delving deep into the Watsons' backgrounds also?"

"We are. Don't worry about that. Is there anything else you can tell us that you neglected to tell the original investigating officer?"

"There's no need to take that tone with me. How many more times do I have to tell you how sorry I am that I didn't speak out? The impact of my silence will live with me for years to come."

"Just answer the question, Mr. Briggs. There's no need to keep repeating yourself. It's my duty as Senior Investigating Officer in charge of a murder enquiry to ask probing questions. That's how we catch ninety-nine percent of the criminals on our radar. Surely you can understand that?"

"I do," he mumbled, reluctantly. "I have nothing further to tell you. May I go now?"

"You may. Can you ask the next person to come in and see us, please? Oh, and here's my card. If you think of anything else I should know about Jamillia, please ring me day or night."

He snatched the card off the desk and pushed back his chair.

Kayli frowned as she watched him storm out of the room. "Anyone would think I spoke harshly to him, but did I?"

Dave shrugged. "No more than usual. You probed, and he got antsy. His problem, not yours I'd say. He was in the wrong for not highlighting possible abuse. Do you think the father is behind this?"

"I'm not sure. It's a tough one. Why didn't Briggs report his conversation with the girl to the head? Too many questions and not enough answers at the moment for my liking, Dave." Kayli smiled as the door opened and a petite woman wearing half-moon glasses walked towards them. "And you are?"

"Mrs. Taylor. I'm one of the longest-serving teachers here at the school."

"Nice to meet you, Mrs. Taylor. What can you tell us about the incident involving Jamillia Watson?"

She shook her head and looked sad. "Nothing really, I'm afraid I was off sick the day she was abducted. I was shocked to see the news last night relating to her death. Such a waste. She was such a happy child."

"We won't keep you long, in that case. We just need to ask everyone what their perception of the child was. You would have had contact with her during break times, I'm presuming. You say she was happy? All the time?"

"I understand. Yes, we all take it in turns to carry out playground duty. I believe she was one of our happier children. She was every time I saw her anyway, although I didn't really have much to do with her, only during playground duties."

"That's right, Mr. Briggs was her teacher. Do you get on well with him?"

The woman's brow furrowed. "Yes, very well. Of course, we don't go out socialising as such. I'm far too busy at home looking after my brood of four to consider doing that kind of thing."

"Four children? Wow, that's brave of you, given the career path you've chosen."

She laughed. "Yes, you're being kind. Most people think I'm just plain stupid when they hear I have four at home as well as looking after a class of twenty-five during the day."

Kayli chuckled. "I can't even begin to imagine how daunting that is. Maybe you can tell me if you saw anyone hanging around the school in the weeks leading up to Jamillia's abduction."

"No. I don't believe so. I'm usually vigilant about things like that when I'm involved in playground duties. We all are, generally. I was surprised to hear that Samantha had let her guard down on that day. That was very remiss of her. I know she's shrouded in guilt now. It must be awful to have a child's death on your conscience."

"I can't even begin to understand how she must be feeling. Is there anything you'd like to add, Mrs. Taylor?"

"I don't think so. Such a shame I was off at the time. I'm a dive-in-and-ask-questions-later type of person. There's no way that bitch would have taken Jamillia on my watch. Sorry for my bad language, but these things infuriate me. It's horrible to think of what the kids go through at the hands of such menaces in society today. Sickening. I don't know how you guys arrest people like this and don't stick the boot in."

Kayli wanted to laugh at the woman's sudden change from meek and mild into vigilante mode but knew she would upset her. "It's hard to show some restraint with certain individuals we arrest. That's for sure." Kayli handed her a card. "Ring me if anything comes to mind that you might have forgotten to tell me. Thanks for talking to us."

Mrs. Taylor pushed back her chair. "I'm sorry I couldn't be of more assistance. I hope you're successful in your hunt for this vile creature and Jamillia gets the justice she deserves."

"Thank you, we hope so too. Can you send in the next teacher please?"

Dave waited until the door shut and then said, "She's right you know. Most coppers would willingly castrate a kiddie fiddler when the bastards are arrested."

"I know, but you're forgetting one vital thing here, Dave."

"What's that?" he asked, tilting his head.

"The kiddie fiddler in this case happens to be female."

"Hmm…you're right. Although, my guess is that a male accomplice was probably driving the van."

"Are you being sexist there? Saying that it's unlikely a woman could have been driving that van?" she teased.

He fidgeted in his chair and glared at her. "Twisting my words again. Shame on you, boss."

"Just teasing. What I am saying is that we need to stick with the facts and not jump ahead of ourselves. Only a few more teachers to interview."

The remainder of the school teachers were interviewed. All of them had taught at the school for years and had never experienced anything such as an abduction of a child before. Though they added nothing further, they were furious and disappointed that Samantha had dropped her guard. Kayli issued each woman a card with clear instructions to contact her straight away if anything sprang to mind.

After completing the interviews, Kayli and Dave sought out the headmistress once more.

"We're all done now," Dave said. "Samantha said that she'd be willing to work with a sketch artist. Would it be okay if that took place here at the school?"

"May I ask why?"

"She lives in a bedsit and thought it would be a little cramped," Kayli offered. "If it's not convenient, I can ask her to come to the station."

"No, here's fine, in that case. Did you discover anything of interest during your chats with the staff?"

"Sadly, not much. It's often difficult to answer questions on the spot. Thank you for allowing us to speak to the staff, though. It truly is much appreciated, Mrs. Laughlin."

"My pleasure. We all want this person caught, as soon as is humanly possible. Good luck with your endeavours."

As they walked out to the car, Dave said, "Let's hope something comes of her dealing with the sketch artist."

Kayli opened the car door and slid behind the steering wheel. "We'll get back to the station and see what the others have come up with in our absence. Then I want to shoot over to Kelvin's place of work and have a word with his boss. In light of what Briggs said, I think we'll have to start looking more at the family."

"I've got my doubts about that one. He didn't seem the type to me."

"Neither to me, but we would be foolish to ignore such an accusation."

## 6

The house was secluded and in the middle of nowhere—where no one would hear the screams. The gang had gathered. Two men and a woman were sitting around the table in the country kitchen that dated back to the fifties.

"We need to get our act together. The police are closing in on us. You screwed up!" Blackbird sneered at Magpie, the only female member of the gang. They made a point of using only nicknames, in case the kids overheard them.

"Fuck you. Like they're gonna find us," she said.

"They will. The police are onto us, I tell you," Blackbird insisted.

"If that's the case, we need to do something to distract them," Swift suggested.

"Yeah, like what?" Magpie asked.

"I haven't thought about that yet."

Blackbird scratched the side of his face and stared at the couple in front of him. He was older than the other two, and more and more, he regretted getting involved with them… especially after Jamillia's death. He'd never had a child die on him before and was disgusted that they'd ruined one of his 'products'.

Magpie sniggered. "Maybe we should nick another one. That would keep the damn cops on their toes."

Blackbird shook his head. "Too soon for that. Why the fuck you had to kill her, I'll never know. What harm was she doing?" His question was aimed at Swift.

"You ain't in charge here. I can do what I friggin' well like."

"At what cost? You need to keep a tight hold on that temper of yours, especially around the kids. You're right, we need to grab another girl to make up the numbers before the big event. But it's too risky to go near a school again. All the teachers in the area are going to be on high alert because *someone* screwed up."

Swift shoved back his chair and got to his feet. "I don't have to take this shit from you, man. It happened—get over it."

"Why did it happen? Because she was black?"

Swift placed his hands on the table and leaned forward until his face was inches from Blackbird's. "If that's what you wanna think, who am I to argue with ya? What's done is done. There's no point dwelling on it. We need to sort out where we go from here. That's what this meeting is about, ain't it?"

"It's about everything. The future, the past and how we're dealing with the girls now. Have they been fed today?"

Swift flung his hands out to the side and paced the floor. "What the fuck do you take me for? Yeah, they were fed first thing."

Blackbird glanced at his watch and shook his head. "Jesus, man. It's almost six now."

"So? Hey, I didn't sign up to this to play nanny to the kids. You guys have gotta pitch in too."

Magpie stood in front of him. "You knew we were both busy. You're the only one out of work."

"Rub it in, why don't ya? Okay, let me take over your job, and you stay here and look after the sprogs instead."

"It ain't gonna happen. It is what it is. It's only going to be for a few more weeks. Just think of what the compensation will be at the end of it."

"It better be worth it. You know I can't be arsed with kids."

"That much is obvious if you haven't fed them. They need three meals a day. You get three meals, don't you?" Blackbird tackled him. "You want them getting sick on us? They'll be worth jack shit if that happens."

"Piss off. I eat when I'm hungry."

"Yeah, but you've got the option. We agreed they should be fed breakfast, lunch and dinner."

"You do it then. I've had it up to here!" Swift jabbed his hand high above his head.

Blackbird withdrew his wallet from his back pocket and threw a twenty-pound note on the table. "Go to the chippy and get five portions of chips."

"What? There's only three of them down there."

"Extra, in case they're hungry. Stop arguing and just do it."

Swift snatched the money and the keys to the van off the table and stormed out of the cottage.

Blackbird glared at Magpie. "He's losing it. You need to have a word. I'm not going to put up with this shit much longer. He either wants the dosh at the end, or tell him to take a hike now."

"I'll have a word later. He's going out of his mind being stuck around here by himself all day."

"Yeah, we all have our crosses to bear. It's for two weeks, maximum. Surely he can put up with this situation for that long?"

"All right. I said I'll deal with it. Back off!"

Blackbird left the table and turned the key to the cellar door. "I'm going to check on them."

"You worry too much. That's your problem," Magpie shouted as he walked down the steps.

Blackbird felt the familiar stirring of excitement creep up his spine as he approached the large cage. The room was dark, except for the shard of light coming from a missing brick in the building's façade. His eyes adjusted quickly and homed in on the three sets of terrified eyes staring back at him. "Hello, girls. How are you doing? I hope you're behaving yourselves."

He watched the girls huddle together, heard their breathing come in fits and starts, the odd gasp now and then as one of them flicked an insect off their skin.

"Please, let us go..."

He peered closer at the girl who had dared to beg. She hid behind one of the other girls.

"You'll be free to go soon. Never fear, little one. Until then, you must remain here, like good little girls. Don't forget, any trouble, and we'll kill your parents. Understand?"

The three horrified girls nodded.

With morbid fascination, he watched their wide eyes fill up with tears then spill over onto their cheeks. "Are you hungry?"

Again, the trio nodded.

"Good, chips are on the way." He moved back towards the stairs and sat on the second step, just watching the girls' reactions to his presence. Something about their fear caused a satisfying glow within him. He strained an ear to hear the crunching of gravel. Not long after, Swift appeared at the top of the stairs.

"Here you are. While you're down there, you might as well feed them yourself."

Blackbird rushed up the stairs and took the hot packages from Swift.

"Get them some water," he ordered, then descended the stairs again to distribute the food.

The bars were too close together for him to pass the packages to the children. He took the key from the hook on the far wall and unlocked the cage. The three girls were too terrified to rush at him to try and escape. They had chosen younger girls who were far more compliant than the older kids he'd dealt with in the past. He entered the cage and presented each of them with a parcel of food. One by one, they grabbed the bundles and ripped them open. He watched with amusement at the way they bolted down the chips, as if they hadn't eaten for days. Perhaps they hadn't. Maybe Swift had lied about feeding them that morning.

Swift appeared behind him with three glasses of water on a small tray. When he walked into the cell, the girls dropped their packages on the floor and clung to each other again. Blackbird's suspicions were raised. *Is he abusing them during the day while I'm at work?* He took the glasses from the tray and distributed them to the girls, then both men left the cage. Blackbird turned the key in the lock and replaced it on the hook. Swift ran up the stairs, eager to get out of the dark cellar, but Blackbird assumed his position on the stairs and watched the starving girls resume their meal with gusto.

# 7

"We're going to call it a day soon," Kayli announced to the team after spending the afternoon going over evidence. "Let's start over in the morning. I think we should begin turning the screws on a few people. In the morning, we need to interview Kelvin Watson's four male friends, shake the tree a bit there, and I want to try and track down his brother Troy, plus visit Kelvin's place of work for a character reference if nothing else."

"What about the alleged abuse by Kelvin?" Dave asked.

"I need to hold fire on that accusation at present. Let's see if we can find out more about Kelvin before we tackle him over that issue. The only way we're going to do that is by interviewing his friends."

The team agreed, all except Dave, but now and then, he was prone to digging his heels in about something. Kayli wondered if he did so intentionally, just to piss her off.

"Also, the sketch artist is due to see Samantha, the teaching assistant at the school tomorrow, so let's hope something comes of that. All right, peeps. Let's call it a day. Well done on what we've managed to achieve so far."

"Goodnight, boss," Donna and Graeme shouted after switching off their computers.

Kayli smiled and waved at them and then turned to Dave who was sitting at his desk lost in thought.

"Something wrong, matey?"

"Not sure. I've got an inkling that we shouldn't delay speaking to the father again. I don't think we should ignore such a vital piece of information that has been handed to us on a plate."

"Dave, I hear you. But, please, let's do things my way. Gather all the evidence we can from his friends, something else might come to light, then we can hit him with the accusations, all in one go."

"Okay, hear me out, boss. The reason I think we should say something now is the fact there is another child in that house—that's my biggest concern."

"Damn, I'd forgotten about that. All right, then maybe you're right. Look, delaying things twenty-four hours won't hurt."

Dave raised his right eyebrow. "Are you seriously willing to take that risk?"

"Sorry, but yes, I am, Dave."

With a shrug, he stood up, slipped on his jacket, and headed for the door. "If anything happens to that little girl, it's on your conscience, not mine. I need to put that on record here."

"Noted. Goodnight, Dave."

He left without responding, leaving Kayli pondering whether she was indeed doing the right thing. She went into her office, picked up her handbag, and switched off the light.

During the drive home, Dave's words constantly filled her head. Kayli pulled up outside her home to hear laughter coming from the lounge. Inserting the key in the front door, she removed her shoes in the hallway and walked into the living room.

"Hello, Giles. This is a surprise. What do we owe the pleasure?" She walked over to her brother and bent down to kiss him on the cheek, then she kissed Mark on the lips. Her fiancé pulled her onto his lap. It felt good to be in his arms after a long day at work.

"Hey, sis, just thought I'd pop in and see how you were both getting on."

"Always good to see you, Giles. Do you want to stay for dinner?"

"Already agreed to, and the dinner is in the oven. Mark and I have had a productive few hours in more ways than one." Giles emptied his can of beer.

"Wow, two surprises in one evening. How will I ever cope? Dare I ask what's on the menu?"

Mark handed her his can of beer. "Pizza and oven chips. Nothing fancy. Good news, love. Giles might have a job for me."

She took a sip from the can then smiled. "Wow, really? What is it?"

Giles tapped the side of his nose, his brown eyes sparkling with amusement. "I need to keep schtum about it for a day or two."

"What? You, secretive little toe rag. Why?"

"Because… stop interrogating me as if I'm one of your suspects. By the way, in all seriousness, how is the case going?"

"Slowly. We questioned everyone at the school today. They're all devastated that Jamillia disappeared under their watch. The poor teaching assistant who virtually handed the little girl over to the perp is mortified. She's been off work for weeks…" She waved her hand in front of her. "Sorry, you don't want to hear about my grim day. When will dinner be ready? Do I have time for a quick shower?"

"Sure, we've got it covered. Should be ten minutes, but we can delay it if you're not down in time."

Kayli kissed Mark and wriggled off his lap. "I'll be down in eight. I'm starving."

After having a swift shower, Kayli rejoined Mark and her brother. One look at the broad smile on her fiancé's face told her that all was not lost for him and their relationship. The man she had fallen in love with a few years ago was still very much there, underneath the heavy layers of self-doubt that had descended upon him of late.

Between them, Giles and Mark entertained her all evening, regaling some of the fun times they had experienced during their spell in the army. Seeing Mark so happy, she wondered if it would have been better for him if he had remained in the army or if there was any way back for him.

At eleven, Giles called a taxi, refusing Kayli's offer to stay in their spare room for the night. She saw him to the front door and lowered

*The Missing Children*

her voice, "Thanks for tonight, love. It was what we both needed. You weren't winding him up about the job, were you?"

Giles kissed her on the cheek. "Hey, you know me better than that, sis. I have a contact getting back to me in a few days. I'll be in touch then. I better go. Annabelle will be wondering where I've got to."

"Give my love to that adorable wife and son of yours. Maybe we can arrange a family barbeque at the weekend or something."

"Sounds like a great idea. I'll have a word with Mum and Dad, see if we can use their gaff. You know how Mum likes to fuss over us."

"Eek... that reminds me, I haven't given them a call in weeks. I'll do it at work tomorrow, if I get the chance."

He walked towards the taxi and called over his shoulder, "They appreciate how busy you are. Don't beat yourself up about that, hon."

"Goodnight, Giles. Thanks again for dropping by. It's always a pleasure seeing my favourite brother."

He laughed. "Your *only* brother. Take care out there, sis."

Kayli blew him a kiss then closed and bolted the front door. When she turned, Mark was standing at the bottom of the stairs, grinning at her.

She sashayed towards him. "Hello, handsome."

He leaned forward, and their lips met in a kiss that took her breath away. Then he grabbed her hand and led her upstairs to bed.

## 8

Kayli left her car and ran for cover in the torrential rain. During her short sprint from the car, the rain soaked through the layers to reach her skin. *Damn! Why did I take my brolly out the car, for fuck's sake?*

She was just shaking the excess rain off her coat when Dave ran through the door behind her. "Bloody hell. What a nightmare of a day. I hope we don't have to go out in that for a while," he said.

Kayli shrugged. "It depends what kind of crap has landed on my desk overnight. Plus, we have all those interviews to conduct today."

"Yeah, I'd forgotten those were on the agenda. We could always invite the men to come down here to speak to us."

"You're impossible, Dave Chaplin. Never thought I'd see the day you were afraid of a drop of rain."

He rushed back to the door and pointed out the pane of glass at the side. "Are you kidding me? A drop of rain? That's bloody monsoon weather out there."

"Hardly. Come on, you wuss."

When they strolled into the incident room, they found Donna with her head in her hands at her computer. Kayli rushed across the room. "Donna, what's wrong?"

The young constable looked up at her and shook her head. "I'm so sorry, boss. I have no idea how I bloody missed it."

Kayli glanced at the screen, and for a second had no idea what she was looking at, but then one name caught her eye. "Shit! Is that what I think it is?"

"Yes, I've been kicking myself for the last twenty minutes, dreading you arriving. I'm sorry."

"What is it?" Dave asked impatiently. He peered over Donna's shoulder and let out a long, low whistle. "Holy crap!"

Kayli dropped into the chair behind her. "Print it out for me, Donna. We need to think about this before we put anything into action."

The printer churned into life and swiftly produced a page. Donna left her seat to collect the sheet and handed it to Kayli. She stared at the information for a few seconds then looked up at Dave. "This should be our first priority today. We need to find Troy Watson."

"I'll get on to his place of work, see what his schedule looks like. He's on the road a lot if I recall, right?" Donna handed him Troy Watson's employment details.

"Yep, tell them it's urgent, that we need to speak to him right away." Kayli smiled at Donna and pointed. "Now don't you dare go blaming yourself. You hear me?"

"But I should have spotted it sooner, boss. When I was carrying out the background checks."

"I've put an awful lot on you in the last few days. Mistakes happen, Donna. We'll put it right, so don't worry. It says here that Troy had a sexual assault charge against him. Look, it could be nothing. If it was against a work colleague, I'm not sure we can link that to the sexual abuse of a child. There again, it's not something we should be ignoring, either. Can you keep digging for me, Donna? Run his name through everything we have and get back to me ASAP."

"I'll do it now, boss."

Kayli walked over to the coffee machine and bought three coffees. She placed one in Donna's hand as she passed and put the other two on the edge of Dave's desk.

Busy talking to someone on the phone, he raised his thumb in appreciation. "Yes, we need to see him urgently. When is he due back in the area?" Not long after, he slammed the phone down and smirked. "The weasel should be at the office around two, the secretary told me."

"Ring her back and tell her to ask him to come in and see us at two thirty, Donna."

"Yes, boss."

"Why the change of heart?" Dave asked.

"Let's try and start twisting the screw. There's no better place to start than with the brother, here on our patch. Until then, let's continue with the plans we put in place yesterday. Donna is doing an in-depth search on Troy now."

Graeme joined them a few minutes later. He apologised for being late and blamed his tardiness on a huge crash he'd encountered on the outskirts of town.

Kayli quickly filled him in on what Donna had discovered. "So that makes Troy our prime suspect, right, boss?"

"Let's just call him 'a person of interest' for now. We still need to arrange the interviews with Kelvin Watson's four friends. Who knows, we could have stumbled on a paedophile ring and find out they're all in on it together, Kelvin, Troy and the four friends for all we know."

Donna gasped. "Your suspected paedophile ring?"

Dave swiftly turned to face Kayli. "You never said you were going down that route?" His tone was brash, as if he were annoyed that Donna knew her suspicions on the case before he'd been privy to the information.

"It was just an assumption I made early on in the case. I had nothing to back up my claims at the time, Dave, and we still haven't, really. Let's just go along with the plan and get these men interviewed today and see where that leads us. I think we should call them in."

"I agree. I'd rather question them here than at their gaffs… although, we *could* use the element of surprise on them and see if they're hiding anything."

"Good point, but without a warrant, we can't go into their homes to snoop around. You know that."

"Yeah, but there are ways to get around that. You could talk to them while I snoop. I could say I need to use the bathroom."

Kayli rolled her eyes. "That old ploy, eh? Okay, let's get these men on the phone and see how things work out. They might prefer to come to the station rather than involve their other halves anyway."

"I'll give them a call and get back to you."

Kayli nodded and took her cup into her office. She sat at her desk just staring at the wall in front of her for a second or two, until she shook herself out of her daydream. Ignoring the pile of post in her in-tray, she rang her mother. "Hello, stranger. Sorry it's been so long since my last call. I've been up to my neck in work."

"Hello, darling. Don't ever worry about that. We're aware of the pressure you're under. Giles told me that you're working that dreadful child murder case. It must be tough on you."

"It is, Mum. Enough talk about work, though. Are you up for a family barbeque soon? Giles is going to call you about it, but I had a spare few minutes, so thought I'd touch base with you first."

"Oh, that would be lovely, sweetheart. Although looking at the downpour we're experiencing today, not sure when we'll be able to fit it in. September is notoriously mixed. No sign of the Indian summer they promised us yet. Typical weathermen getting it wrong again. Let's play it by ear for the moment. Say yes for now, but subject to change."

"I know what you mean. I got drowned just running from the car into the station this morning. Okay, I'll leave it with you then, Mum. Call me if you need a hand with anything, although you know I'm not that handy in the kitchen, so maybe it would be better if you asked Annabelle to help you in that department."

They both laughed then hung up.

Dave appeared in the doorway a few moments later. "They've all agreed to come in during the day, three of them during lunch. We might have to split up to question them, and the fourth said he can call in after work around five fifteen. I said that was fine."

"Great stuff. Okay, let's spend the morning delving into their backgrounds, ensure we don't miss anything."

"I'm on it now."

She clicked her fingers together. "I know what I've forgotten to do. Ring Kelvin and Lorella's bosses. I'll rectify that now."

"Good idea. I'll leave you to it."

Kayli looked up the number for Crazy Joe's Place and the Co-op store and decided to call the Co-op first. "Hello, this is DI Bright from the Avon and Somerset Constabulary. Is it possible to have a chat with the manager please?"

"Just a moment. I'll see if he's free," a woman replied.

Kayli waited on hold, listening to a classical music clip, which she found surprisingly soothing. *Hmm... maybe I should get some of this for the car. Never liked the stuff before, but this is pretty cool. Maybe I'm mellowing with age!*

"Hello, Trevor Stott speaking. What can I do for you, Inspector?"

"Hello, sir. I appreciate you taking my call. It's just a general enquiry really. I'm the officer in charge of the Jamillia Watson murder case and wondered if you could give me some background information on her mother, Lorella."

"I'm not following you, Inspector. What could I possibly tell you that you think will help you with your case? Are you saying that Lorella is involved in her daughter's murder?"

"No, not in the slightest. Sorry if I gave you that impression. I just need to ask how she is at work. Any complaints about her from customers, perhaps?"

"Nothing. Nothing at all. Lorella is considered to be a valued member of our team. Although she is part-time, she often stays on longer when one of her colleagues is running late. Not many people do that nowadays, I can tell you."

"Thank you. That's all I needed to hear. I appreciate your time, Mr. Stott." Kayli hung up and dialled the number for Crazy Joe's Place.

"Hi, Crazy Joe's Place. How may I help you?"

"Hi, I'm Detective Inspector Bright. Is it possible to speak to the manager please?"

"He's just here. Hold the line."

There was a click on the line as the call was transferred. "Hello, this is the manager, Mr. Parsons. What can I do for you?"

*The Missing Children*

"Hello, I'm the investigating officer in the Jamillia Watson murder enquiry. I understand her father, Kelvin, works for you."

He gasped. "Yes, he does. Oh dear, that was a dreadful piece of news to hear. We're all devastated here. Kelvin and Lorella are such devoted parents. What sort of information do you need?"

"Mainly about Kelvin. I need to know what kind of character he is. Whether he has any problems at work, any complaints against him from the customers. That type of thing."

"I see. Well, he's one of my best employees. He's won employee of the month six times already this year. As far as I can remember, he's never had an argument with a customer or had a complaint filed against him. I wish I employed a dozen more like him. It would make my working life a whole lot easier."

"That's reassuring to know."

"You think he's involved in this deplorable crime?"

"No. Nothing like that. We're just building a picture, that's all. Looking along the lines that maybe he'd fallen out with someone at work or a punter and they'd taken revenge on his family."

"Oh Lordy! I never even thought about that. Let me have a proper think… no, still nothing coming to mind, I'm sorry. I wish I could help you more. The person who did that to their darling daughter needs stringing up. They should bring back capital punishment for people involved in murdering kids. There's just no deterrent in this day and age. A life means nothing."

"I see you're pretty irate about the system, Mr. Parsons."

"And some, Inspector. Every time you turn on the news, there's yet another one of these crimes being talked about. Look at that case with that depraved bastard who used to work for the Beeb. How the hell did that man get away with that level of abuse? Oh, sorry, don't get me started. He was filth, and yet he was given privilege passes to go and see kids that were dying—in some cases, only to abuse them. What kind of sick fucker does that? And to be allowed to get away with it for decades, and to have been made a Sir! That's simply unforgiveable."

"I agree totally, which is why I'm ringing up today to see if there is any information about Kelvin that you might think would be useful going forward in the case."

"Ahh... I'm with you now. Seriously, Inspector, you couldn't wish for a nicer chap. I promise you. Nicer couple even. On his days off, he used to bring Jamillia and Marcia in for a burger. Jamillia was keen to see where her daddy worked. Such an adorable child. Such a waste."

"We're doing our best to get the little girl and her family justice. I can promise you that. Thank you for your time, Mr. Parsons."

"Do it for all of us, Inspector. We're standing strong behind the distraught family."

"We will, sir. Goodbye."

Kayli spent the rest of the morning popping in and out of the office, chasing her team for any new leads in between dealing with her daily chores. Dave surprised her with a sandwich at around twelve, then he sat down in the chair opposite and tucked into his own.

"Thought we better have some grub before the first interviewee arrives. He's due at twelve thirty."

"I needed this. Anything else come to light out there?"

"Nothing yet. Donna is still beside herself for messing up with Troy Watson."

"These things happen. She needs to stop blaming herself. At least she made amends early. I can't wait to question Troy Watson."

"Don't you think it's strange that Kelvin didn't tell us about his brother's assault charge?"

"Maybe he doesn't know about it," Kayli replied, sinking her teeth into her tuna-and-mayo wholemeal sandwich.

"We'll soon find out. How are we going to play it with the other four men?"

Kayli sipped her coffee. "Shall we take two each?"

"I don't mind. How far do you want me to go with them?"

"Just ask the basic questions. How often they socialised with the family? Have they ever witnessed anything between the parents and the children that raised their suspicions? Then turn the tables on them, ask them if Jamillia had ever confided in either them or their partners. How they interacted with the little girl and her sister? Do they have kids of their own? Did their kids ever play with the Watson children? If they did, where did they play? Have their children ever indicated that Jamillia was concerned at home?

"I rang Kelvin and Lorella's places of employment this morning and asked pretty much the same kind of thing. Both managers assured me they are decent people who idolise their kids. I still have this niggling doubt about what was planted by the teacher, though. We need to follow up on that."

"You think we should go and see the parents again? Ask the father outright about those claims?"

"Maybe."

"Someone must know something. It's just finding that person. You really think we could be looking at a paedophile ring here?"

Kayli sighed. "I'm not a hundred percent sure of that, but consider how many children have gone missing in the past few months."

Dave fell silent and finished off his sandwich. The phone on her desk rang. It was the desk sergeant, who informed her that the first interviewee had arrived.

Dave jumped out of his chair. "You finish your lunch. I'll grab this one."

"Thanks, I appreciate it. Don't forget, be nice in there, Dave. No one is a suspect yet. If anything comes to light during the interviews, then we'll haul their arses back in and twist the screw, all right?"

Dave saluted from the doorway. "I hear you."

Kayli nibbled a few more mouthfuls of her sandwich then pushed it aside. Moments later, the desk sergeant rang to say that the second interviewee was waiting in the reception area for her. She finished her coffee and rushed down the stairs, notebook in hand, to meet Desmond Jensen. He was a tall, athletically built black man who was quietly spoken. The interview was painless enough. He told her that he'd never been left alone with either of the Watsons' children and had only visited the house a few times with his family. Most of the time, the three other friends who were being interviewed met up with Kelvin now and again on a night out down the pub. Nowadays, such events were happening less and less as everyone's family expanded.

"Have you ever had any reason to suspect either of the Watsons to be abusing their children?"

He shook his head at the same time his eyes bulged. "I'm actually appalled that you should suggest such a thing. I've never even heard either of them raise their voice in anger at the kids, not that they were bad kids."

"Okay, that concludes the interview. I really appreciate you coming to see me today during your lunch hour."

"Anything to help, Inspector. But if you're going along the lines that the Watsons could be guilty of killing their own child, then I'm begging you to reconsider that scenario. There is no way they'd ever harm a hair on either of their children's heads. It's unthinkable, in fact."

"All we're doing at the moment is dotting the i's and crossing the t's, Mr. Jensen. I'm sure the facts will reveal themselves shortly. In the meantime, we have to keep digging with the evidence we have to hand."

"I understand. You have a tough job, and I don't envy you in the slightest. Goodbye, Inspector, and good luck." He rose from his seat and shook her hand.

Kayli walked him back up the corridor to the main entrance, and as Dave was obviously still occupied with his interviewee, she collected the third friend, Warren Northcott. He was muscular and had the darkest skin she'd ever laid eyes on. The whites of his eyes were like beacons, drawing her in. The interview again turned out to be fruitless. Warren virtually reiterated what Desmond had told her. Feeling discouraged, she ended the interview and said farewell to Warren at the main entrance. She returned to the incident room to find Dave sitting at his desk, looking equally disappointed.

"Well, that was a complete waste of time. I take it was the same for you?" he asked, throwing a pen across his desk.

Kayli propped her backside on the desk closest to her partner. "We've still got the other friend coming in this evening and Troy to question in half an hour or so. That should prove to be more interesting. At least, I'm hoping it will be."

"It better be. The longer this takes, I feel as though we're letting the kids down."

Kayli rubbed his upper arm. "I know, mate. We'll catch a break soon. I'm sure."

"I bloody well hope so; it's starting to affect my sleep. If they're still out there, no one knows the perils that lie ahead of these kids. They must be bloody petrified."

She saw his eyes puddle with tears and wanted to reach out and give him a cuddle. She held back as a lump the size of an orange surfaced in her own throat. "I know I don't have any kids of my own, Dave. It doesn't mean that I'm affected any less by this."

"I know. I wasn't insinuating that, boss. Merely venting my frustrations. Maybe we should start checking out all the derelict buildings in the area, after all?"

"Let's see how the final two interviews go first, and we'll debate what to do next afterwards. How's that?"

He shrugged. "You're the boss."

Donna answered the phone ringing on her desk, said thank you, and hung up. "Boss, Troy Watson is waiting in reception for you."

"Here we go. Are you ready for this, Dave?"

"As I'll ever be. Let's go rattle his cage."

When Kayli first laid eyes on Troy Watson, he was wearing a deeply engrained frown. She offered her hand for him to shake, but he refused.

"If you'd like to follow us into the interview room," Kayli said calmly.

"Do I have a choice?" the man grumbled as he followed her into the room.

"No," Dave confirmed, bringing up the rear.

Kayli and Dave sat on one side of the table, and she motioned for Troy to sit opposite them. "We're going to tape this interview, if that's okay?"

"I thought this was just an informal chat. Now you're stating it's an interview. What about my rights? Am I not entitled to have my solicitor present with me? Although why this has turned into an interview is beyond me. What gives, Inspector? Have I done something wrong?"

"If you want a solicitor to be present that is entirely up to you, Mr. Watson. We can delay the interview until you make the arrangements for your solicitor to come over, or we can continue now and get this over and done with as soon as possible. The choice is yours."

"You think by pinning me in a corner, I'll drop a clanger and reveal something? I know how these things work, Inspector. You may look cute, but it's not the smartest move you've ever made." He folded his arms, forming a barrier between them. "I want my solicitor here, now."

"And who might that be, Mr. Watson?"

"Roger Moorcroft of Taylor and Moorcroft."

"Dave, would you mind placing the call for me?"

Dave turned to face her, his expression full of concern.

"Mr. Watson and I will be fine until you return."

"If you're sure. I'll go and call him now."

Troy snorted. "What? You think I'd be foolish enough to attack her?"

Dave glared at Watson before he rushed out of the room.

Kayli didn't feel threatened in the slightest in Dave's absence. She fiddled around with the tape machine, ensuring it was ready, as a distraction to combat the silence that had descended in the room. Dave returned within minutes.

"Moorcroft will be here in fifteen minutes. Luckily, he was having an admin day, therefore, he didn't have to postpone any of his clients. You're a lucky man."

Troy Watson grinned. "That's me all over. I was born lucky, man."

The room remained silent until there was a rap on the door, and Roger Moorcroft entered the room, carrying his briefcase. "Sorry for the delay. I'm Roger Moorcroft. May I ask what this interview is regarding?"

Kayli and Dave shook the solicitor's hand.

"We're interviewing everyone connected to the Watson family after the discovery of Jamillia Watson's body," Kayli said. "Your client has been away from home for a number of days, and therefore, we've been

*The Missing Children*

unable to reach him. However, after doing some background checks, we've uncovered something in your client's background that has flagged up a concern for us. I would rather we said anything further while the tape is running, if that's okay with you?"

"I see. Very well, Inspector. Go for it." He turned to face his client, giving him a smug smile. That action alone made Kayli's skin crawl, making her ponder if the solicitor was covering up something worse than they already suspected.

Dave reeled off the relative information for the tape and also added that both audio and visual evidence could be used at a later date if needed.

Kayli cleared her throat. "Okay, first of all, what can you tell me about the disappearance of your niece, Jamillia, Mr. Watson?"

His mouth twisted and he tilted his head. "Are you serious? Why the fuck would I know anything about it?"

"Just answer the question," Dave prompted harshly.

"Nothing. I was as distraught about the situation as Kelvin and Lorella were."

"Did you go to the house to comfort either of them?"

"No. I contacted them by telephone. I have a hectic job. I'm on the road most of the time. I catch up with my family only when time permits. My job means everything to me."

"It must have come as a shock when you had the charge laid at your door then. You know, the sexual assault charge."

His chest inflated, and his arms rose and fell a few times. "What the fuck has that got to do with anything? I hope you're not suggesting what I think you are."

Kayli shrugged. "You seem an intelligent man, Mr. Watson. You tell us if there's a connection here. You must be aware of your niece's injuries."

He shook his head adamantly, chewed the inside of his mouth, and narrowed his eyes. "I'm aware that she suffered some form of abuse. Kelvin kept the facts from me because he said they were too gruesome to mention to anyone else. You're friggin' sick if you think I'd do that to my own niece."

"Am I? Why don't you tell us how the charges against you came about then? I'm sure we're all dying to hear."

He let out a large breath. "That charge was years ago, and it was dropped. Did you neglect to read that part of the file, Inspector?"

"I read it. Still, it was necessary to ask you about the incident. So, in your own words, how did the incident occur?"

"Jesus, really? Can she do this?" he pleaded with his solicitor.

Moorcroft looked up from his legal pad and shrugged. "Just answer her. If you don't, they'll only think you've got something to hide."

"Christ! That's your professional advice? Well, for the record, I think it sucks. Just like you bringing up a charge that was dropped almost six years ago. Does this mean it's going to be permanently on my record? Isn't there a law against that?"

"No law against it, Mr. Watson. Just answer the question," Dave said, crossing his arms.

He clawed at the side of his face with his right hand. "This is unbelievable. All right, it happened at a staff Christmas party—there's a surprise, right? You know, when the drink was flowing nice and fast and everyone's inhibitions got lost in the moment. The woman came onto me. When I refused to visit the toilets with her for the shag that was on offer, she started screaming and telling everyone that I had touched her up. I did no such bloody thing. You read it all the time in the newspaper—you know, women crying wolf when they can't get what they want. Well, that's what happened with me. And yeah, the mud stuck with me for months. No, make that a few friggin' years. Because yet again, the incident has reared its ugly head now. I repeat, the charges were dropped. The slag admitted that she wanted me and I'd refused to entertain her."

Kayli nodded and asked, "When were the charges dropped?"

"She let me friggin' sweat it out for three whole months before she admitted her allegation was false to another colleague who was also a good friend of mine. That friend went straight to my boss, and the bitch broke down into tears when the boss confronted her. She left the company that day—resigned she did. Although, I think the boss more than likely gave her an ultimatum. I was innocent that night at the party and have never, ever been guilty of touching either a woman or child inappropriately in my life. I can't believe you would suggest such a thing. Wait a minute... or has someone dropped a hint in your ear? Like my brother, perhaps? Has he put you up to this?"

"No. We're just making general enquiries. Does your brother know about the sexual assault charge?"

Troy sighed. "None of my family know. They don't need to know about that, either."

"Had you been here a few hours earlier you would have seen Kelvin's friends in the reception area, waiting to be interviewed. As I've already stated, we're questioning everyone connected to Kelvin, Lorella, or their children."

"Have you grilled the parents?" Troy demanded angrily.

"Is there a reason why you should ask that?"

"Just going along the lines you've outlined. How many of these cases end up in the news, pointing the finger at the parents? I love my brother dearly, but do we truly know what goes on behind closed doors, Inspector?"

Dave nudged her knee with his under the table.

Kayli sighed. "Is that truly what you think?"

"Maybe they disguise it well until the front door is firmly shut," he said bitterly.

"Are you perhaps just striking out because you think your brother has pointed us in your direction?"

"If the cap fits. Who knows nowadays? If he's keen to point the finger at me, I'm more than willing to return the compliment."

Kayli raised her eyebrows. "Family loyalty, eh? There's nothing like it."

"Are we done here now, Inspector?" Moorcroft said, tapping his pen on his notebook.

"I think so. Unless there is anything else your client wants to tell us?"

"Nothing. I know nothing about my niece's abduction or her death. I want to put it on record that I think it's appalling that you should order me in here for questioning like this when you should be out there trying to find the real culprit. Clutching at straws comes to mind, Inspector."

"Thank you for humouring us in that case, Mr. Watson. I'd rather clutch at straws than have the culprit hiding under our radar. As you said earlier, a lot of these types of crimes reported through the media reveal the murderers to be the parents or even a relative. I like to think of us covering our backs. If we offend the family members along the way, then that's something we're all going to have to live with. I appreciate you taking the time to come and see me."

"Huh! Typical woman! Seems to me like you've got an answer for everything."

She scowled at him as Dave ended the interview for the tape. Kayli and Dave walked the two men back through the reception area and tried to shake their hands. Moorcroft accepted, though Troy Watson merely looked at them in disgust.

Kayli smiled at the solicitor and said, "You have my card. Please get in touch if you think of anything else we should know in the future."

After the men left, Kayli and Dave walked slowly back up the stairs to the incident room.

"What did you make of him?" Dave asked.

"He seemed genuine enough. Maybe it was wrong to haul him in and throw the assault charge at him. He's right—that type of thing shouldn't see the light of day once the charges have been dropped."

"Yeah, I can see his point of view, but it's always going to be on his record, boss. He needs to deal with it. Perhaps it'll keep him in line in the future, not that he's guilty of doing anything, but it might act as a deterrent if the temptation arises in years to come."

Kayli's lip curled and her brow furrowed. "Are you bloody talking in riddles again, Dave?"

"I know what I mean. I just didn't articulate it very well, I guess."

"No shit, Sherlock! You are funny. Seriously, though, I think we can discount him, but what we can't dismiss is what he and the teacher have both suggested."

"The teacher maybe. I wouldn't necessarily let what Troy said about his brother cloud your judgement, boss. It reeks of a tit-for-tat ploy to me."

Kayli chewed her lip the rest of the way into the incident room, contemplating her partner's warning. The team spent the afternoon going over and over old ground. Kayli felt they were no closer to discovering who had abducted the girls or who had tortured and killed little Jamillia Watson. Her gut told her that none of her family members were capable of such deplorable behaviour. *But if it wasn't them, then who?*

However, after getting nowhere with the final interviewee, who turned up at five fifteen as promised, she took the decision to visit the Watsons with Dave in the early evening, not knowing if Kelvin would be home or not.

## 9

Kelvin opened the door, his expression confused. "Hello, Inspector. What are you doing here?"

"All right if we come in for a moment, Kelvin? There are a few things we need to clarify."

He stood aside to let them into the house. He motioned for them to go in the lounge, where they found Lorella, still in her dressing gown, playing with Marcia on the floor. Lorella jumped to her feet and gripped her gown tightly at her chest.

"Hello, do you have some news for us? Have you found him?" Lorella asked, her eagerness noticeable in her high-pitched voice.

Kelvin walked across the room and placed an arm around his wife's shoulders.

"Maybe we should do this without your daughter being in the same room," Kayli suggested with a taut smile.

Lorella looked at her husband, panic-stricken.

"Please, just say what you have to say. Marcia is distracted with her toys—aren't you, darling?" Kelvin asked, looking down at his daughter, who was humming to herself and playing with her dolls.

When Marcia didn't answer her father, or acknowledge the officers, Kayli thought it would be okay to proceed. "We've gone through the list of names you gave us and interviewed everyone concerned. A few things were highlighted by your friends that I'd like to address, if that's all right with you?"

"Okay, would it be better if we sat down for this?" Kelvin suggested.

The four of them sat down, and Kayli's gaze drifted towards Marcia again. "First of all, Kelvin, I need you in particular to remain calm whilst I tell you what one of Jamillia's teachers told us. It seems that your daughter had confided in them a few weeks before her disappearance."

Kelvin and Lorella exchanged confused glances.

"Confided what?" Kelvin asked eventually.

"The teacher said that Jamillia told them you had touched her inappropriately." Kayli's gaze swiftly shifted between Marcia and her parents. The little girl, thankfully, continued to be mesmerised with her toys in her own little world.

Kelvin jumped off the couch and ran a hand over his short hair. "What? This is crazy. I would never, *never* do such a thing." He looked over at his wife.

Her mouth was hanging open, and she was staring up at him.

"Lorella, you have to believe me."

Lorella began to slowly shake her head as tears dripped onto her cheek. "Why? Why would she tell someone that if it wasn't true, Kelvin? Answer me that!" She dropped onto the floor and cradled her daughter in her arms.

"Are you telling us that it's a lie, Kelvin?" Kayli prompted.

"Yes. Yes, it's a damn lie, but how am I going to prove it now my daughter is dead. Who said this? I need to have a word with them, the twisted shit."

"I'm not at liberty to reveal that. They were adamant that Jamillia confided in them, but the conversation was not reported to the headmistress."

"So, someone hints at something that can neither be proven nor disproven, and you think it's all right to come here to my home and cast your aspersions?"

"No one has done anything of the sort. If a statement such as this is highlighted during an investigation, then I am duty bound to ask you whether the allegation was true or not."

"Well, it *wasn't*. Jesus, I can't believe Jamillia would ever tell anyone such a downright lie. Why? Why would she say that about me? I loved the very bones of that girl. I protected her when she was in my care. Never once did I touch her in the wrong way. I can't believe that she would even suggest such a disgusting thing. Why would she say that, Lorella?"

His wife rocked their daughter and stared at him through wide eyes.

"My God, don't tell me you believe this crap? You know me better than that."

He paced the floor as his anxiety mounted.

"I thought I did..." Lorella replied quietly.

Kayli's heart thundered. She despised putting the family through such angst at a time when they were busy grieving for their daughter. Nothing in what Kelvin had said or done so far had caused her to doubt he was telling the truth. "Like I say, it's just an allegation at this point."

Kelvin threw himself back into his chair. "What does that mean? Are you saying that you believe me? Because if you are, I wish you'd tell my wife that. I think she suspects that I'm some kind of monster right now."

With the raised voices between her parents, Marcia started to cry. His wife shot him a distrustful glance but said nothing as she soothed their daughter with a rocking motion.

"I needed to make you aware of what had been said. There's no way of us telling if this is a false accusation or not, as your daughter is no longer around to verify the claim."

"I'm telling you, Inspector, it's a downright lie and one that has made me sick to my stomach. Who could make up such a lie about me? Is it that easy to convince the cops these days? One allegation—a *false* allegation!—and you begin to treat someone you've been dealing with in a different way."

"That really isn't going to happen, Mr. Watson. I'll note the information down, but at this point, I have no intention of taking things further."

"Are you saying that you won't be involving Social Services?" Lorella asked in a shaky voice.

"No. I see no reason to. I just wanted to make you both aware of what had been said. I have another snippet of news to tell you that you might not want to hear."

Kelvin threw his hands up in the air. "Great, hit us with more bad news, why don't you? Keep piling it on us, making us feel worse still."

"I need to reassure you that it's nothing to do with you directly, if that puts your mind at rest."

"Okay, let's hear it."

"We had to call your brother in for questioning because we discovered a sexual assault charge in your brother's file." Kayli raised her hand when she saw Kelvin's agitation. "I have to say in your brother's defence, the charge was later dropped."

"Bloody hell. When?"

"A few years ago. Obviously, in a case such as this, that type of information can be seen as crucial to the SIO. Having spoken to your brother for a few hours, I'm satisfied that no further action needs to be taken against him."

"So why bring it up?" Lorella asked. "Do you like causing us misery intentionally?"

"Sorry, that was not my intention. I needed to tell you the truth of where we are at this point in the investigation."

"But he never told us," Kelvin said, shaking his head in disbelief. "Why? Who accused him of the assault? Was it a child?"

"No. The allegation was raised by one of his work colleagues. It wouldn't be right of me to continue the investigation without you being aware of that information. The charge was dropped before it got out of hand."

"But you believe there's no smoke without fire, right?"

"Maybe. What I wanted to ask, is if you've ever had any reason to distrust your brother around either of your children."

"No, never. Christ, we're a loving family. We've never had any reason to suspect any family members of…well, you know, that *filth*. We're an ordinary family whose child was abducted from somewhere she should have been safe. Now all this shit is coming to our door. I'm at a loss what to say about this, Inspector. You say the charges were dropped against my brother, and yet, here you are bringing them to our attention. I can only assume that you think he's involved with Jamillia's abduction in some way."

"No, I genuinely don't. I'm sorry. I just felt you needed to know the facts. I really didn't want to add to your burden at this sad time. If you'd rather me not update you on how the investigation is progressing, then that's fine by me." Kayli rose from her chair, and Dave followed her out into the hallway.

Kelvin joined them and opened the front door. "I'm not sure how you expected me to react to such news, Inspector. I'm sorry if your visit didn't go as you planned."

"It doesn't matter, Mr. Watson. I want to assure you that we will be noting down the accusation from the teacher but not taking it further at this point. If some other evidence shows up in the meantime, then I might have to revisit that decision later."

Kelvin let out a large sigh. "So be it. I suppose I should be grateful to you for at least not arresting me and hauling my arse down the station. Please keep us informed of what you find, Inspector. I promise to try and not overreact next time."

She held out her hand for him to shake. "Your reaction was understandable. Had you not reacted in the way you did, it would have caused major suspicions in my mind. Look at it as you passing a test."

Kelvin smiled. "Thanks, I think. Good luck with your investigation."

They left the house and jumped back in the car.

"What did you make of that?" Dave asked.

"Nothing to make of it. He's innocent in my eyes. What I really want to know is why Jamillia confided in her teacher the way she did?"

"Confided or lied?"

"Either she lied or Briggs is lying. But why?"

She dropped Dave back at the station and noted the time on the dashboard. It was almost six thirty, later than usual for her to be going home. She rang Mark en route to see if he wanted her to pick up a take-away. He sounded almost distant on the phone. Gone was the joviality of the previous day. She couldn't help wondering if Giles's promise of the possibility of a job offer had fallen through, like so many others.

*Ever the pessimist, love. Keep up the good work.* She chastised herself as she queued up for fish and chips at the nearby chippie.

When she arrived home, Mark had the plates laid out on the kitchen table and had opened a bottle of wine. He ate his meal without any reference to his job hunting, and Kayli didn't have the heart to raise the subject as they snuggled up together on the couch to watch an action movie they had seen half a dozen times before. It felt good to be wrapped in his arms, setting aside the mixed day she'd had at work and his lack of news on the job front. Over dinner they shared their excitement about the forthcoming barbeque at the weekend. Maybe Giles would be able to give them more details about the job he hinted at by then. For now, it felt good to be snuggled up, ignoring all that was wrong in their lives.

## 10

*D*uring her drive into work, Kayli switched on the car radio just in time to catch a report about a fire at the Watsons' address. She turned up the volume at the same time she pressed her foot down on the accelerator and dipped down a side road. *A fire. Shit!*

Within five minutes, she had parked her vehicle in the station car park and was running up the staircase to the incident room. Donna was sitting at her desk, sipping a cup of coffee.

"Have you heard the news?" Kayli asked her.

Looking puzzled, Donna shook her head. "No, boss. About what?"

"A fire, at the Watsons' house! I just heard it on the radio in the car. Can you get me more information about it?"

"On it now, boss. Shit! That doesn't sound good."

Kayli glanced at the clock on the wall. Almost eight forty-five. "Come on, Dave. Get your arse in here." She paced the floor for the next five minutes to the sound of Donna pounding the keys on her keyboard.

Dave walked into the office soon after. "Morning all. Something wrong, boss?"

"Damn right it is. We need to get over there, now!"

"Whoa, back up a second. Where?"

Kayli ran an agitated hand over her face. "The Watsons'—I need to see for myself what happened."

"There's been a fire, Dave," Donna said, filling in the gap.

"Shit! Okay, we need to get there ASAP, boss. I'll drive. You're in no fit state."

Kayli's heart was in her mouth as she arrived at the scene. Warrant card in hand, she approached the fireman who appeared to be in charge. "Hi, I'm DI Kayli Bright. Can you tell me what happened? Are the family all right?" she asked as she read the graffiti that had been daubed across the front of the Watsons' house. *Child killers! Rot in hell.* The window to the lounge had shattered, but that was the extent of the damage from what Kayli could tell.

"Yes, luckily, the father got all three of them out before the fire had a chance to spread inside. Judging by the message scrawled across the front of the house, I take it the fire was started intentionally."

"The couple's daughter was found murdered a few days ago."

"I see. Looks like someone squirted petrol through the letterbox then threw a lighted match in to ignite it."

Kayli searched the area. "And the family? Where are they now?"

"They were whisked away in an ambulance. Suffering from smoke inhalation."

"Damn! Let's hope it's nothing serious."

"The fire didn't get a chance to get out of hand. I think they'll be fine. We got here as fast as we could."

"What time did this occur?"

"Around six this morning."

"Wow, okay. Thanks for all your help. I'm going to shoot over to the hospital now." She smiled and ran back towards the car, where Dave was standing. "Let's get to the hospital. See how this went down."

Dave drove and Kayli leapt out of the car before it had even stopped. She heard Dave's footsteps behind her as she entered the reception area of the hospital. Flashing her ID, she asked, "A family were caught in a fire. Can you tell me where I'm likely to find them?"

The brunette smiled and looked down at her computer monitor. "Do you have a name I can search for?"

"Sorry, Kelvin and Lorella Watson, and their daughter Marcia."

"Ah, yes. They're still in A&E, being processed."

Kayli pointed left and right with her hands. "Which way?"

"To the right, just down the hallway."

"Thanks. Come on, Dave."

They rushed through the busy hallway and into the Accident and Emergency Department, where they found yet another brunette sitting at a desk. Kayli showed her warrant card again. "Kelvin and Lorella Watson, where are they?"

"In the cubicles on the left. I'll get someone to show you through."

"No, it's fine. I'll find them." She rushed towards the cubicles and called out, "Kelvin, are you here?"

"In here," a croaky voice replied.

Dave poked his head round the nearest curtain. "Hello, mate. How are you doing?"

Kayli followed her partner into the cubicle. Kelvin was sitting on the bed, fully clothed, looking bewildered. "I'm fine. We're all fine, I think."

"Can you tell us what happened?" Kayli walked around the other side of the bed and stood beside him.

"It's all such a blur. I was asleep on the couch. I was on the nightshift, and the boss sent me home early. I couldn't concentrate at work after the conversation we'd had yesterday. I only got home at five thirty. I dread to think what might have happened to Lorella and Marcia if I'd stayed at work. Why would anyone do this to us? We're just a normal family grieving the loss of our beautiful daughter. Why punish us further by destroying our home? Did you see what they wrote on our house? Is that what we're going to have to put up with for the rest of our lives? Is that what people truly believe?" He coughed, having used up all the breath in his lungs.

"First of all, I have to say, I'm so sorry that this has happened. People always react badly where children are concerned. Thank God you were at home to save Lorella and Marcia."

"That's what keeps going over and over in my mind. Would they have survived if I hadn't been there? I don't believe they would have. Lorella was out cold, as she'd taken a sleeping tablet." He covered his face with his hands and sobbed. "Jesus, if I hadn't left work early, I would now be grieving the loss of all of my family... not just Jamillia. Why?"

Kayli and Dave looked at each other. *What is this really about? A vendetta of sorts?* "Kelvin, you have to think, deep into the recesses of your mind... can you come up with anyone who could have a possible vendetta against you? Anything at all?"

He dropped his hands from his face and swiped at the tears. "I've thought long and hard about that very thing, but I can't think of anyone who would be that callous to have done such a thing. They'd need to have a badly twisted mind, and no one I know comes close to that."

Kayli placed a hand on his arm. "Just keep thinking, all right? Something doesn't stack up here."

"I've never knowingly fallen out with anyone in my life. Even if I had, would they truly come after me and my kids in this dreadful way?"

"In our experience, it only takes a minor incident to trigger some people off. Keep mulling things over."

"I'm thinking of nothing else. Can you have a word with the doc for me? I need to see my family."

Kayli nodded and left the cubicle. A doctor was talking to a nurse outside a cubicle farther down the hallway. She fished out her ID again and showed it to him. "Hello, Doc. I'm investigating the crime against the Watson family. Can you tell me how they are?"

"Very lucky. Although the child is suffering more than the adults from smoke inhalation. We've moved her to ICU as a precaution so we can keep a close eye on her."

"Is she going to be okay?"

"Hopefully, yes. But we won't be able to tell how much damage has been done for a day or two. We'll monitor her vital signs until then. Mrs. Watson has been transferred to the women's ward. She's asleep, I believe. It's my understanding that she had taken a sleeping tablet last night, so she's very fortunate that her husband saved her. They both are. He's a very brave man."

"He is. He loves his family. That much is clear. Thanks, Doc." Kayli returned to the cubicle to find both Kelvin and Dave waiting patiently for the update. "Your wife has been moved to the women's ward, and she's asleep. Marcia has been transferred to ICU as a precaution. She's having a hard time breathing on her own at present. She'll be well cared for up there."

Kelvin swivelled and dropped his legs to the floor. "I need to go and see her. Them. Please help me?"

"It would be better to stay here until the doctor discharges you, Kelvin. There's nothing you can do for either of them at this time."

The curtain swished, and the doctor Kayli had spoken to in the hallway entered the cubicle. "I understand your need to be with your family, Mr. Watson. Let me give you a final once-over, and then you're free to go, okay?"

Kayli gestured for Dave to leave them to it. In the hallway, she ran a concerned hand through her hair. "We need to get back to the station to begin the investigation, but I don't want it to feel as though we're running out on him at a time when he needs our support."

"His family are safe in the hospital. We should get back. We can't catch the bastards who did this hanging around here."

"I know. Let's see what the doc says first and then decide. What a bloody mess."

"Hey, I know that look. Don't you go thinking we're to blame for this."

"What if one of his neighbours did it? What if they saw us at his house and presumed he was guilty?"

Dave shrugged. "Even if they did, that's still no excuse to try and kill the family. You know it takes a certain type of person to want to kill someone, boss."

"Right. But we haven't questioned any of the neighbours. Maybe that's where we've been going wrong."

"Hmm... Want me to ring the station and get it organised?"

"No. I think we should return to the scene and question the neighbours ourselves."

"Boss, you can't do everything yourself. I know how much you hate to delegate, but—"

"We're doing it. That's the end of it, Dave."

The doctor and Kelvin walked out of the cubicle. "I've given him the all-clear under strict instructions that if he feels worse, he immediately reports back to me and my team," the doctor informed them before he walked away.

"Excellent news. Are you going to sit with your daughter, Kelvin?"

"Yes, I need to be with her. I can't stand the thought of losing another daughter. Who would try and kill us like this? We've never knowingly fallen out with anyone. Who could think we'd be responsible of murdering our own daughter?"

Kayli's heart squeezed. She placed a comforting hand on his arm. "We're going to do our very best to find out. We're heading off soon. Are you sure you're going to be okay? Shall we come with you to ICU?"

"No, I can manage. I'd rather you be out there, looking for the person who tried to destroy my family. Do you think it's the same person who abducted Jamillia? It wasn't enough for them to put us through the turmoil of losing one child so they returned to ensure we suffered the loss of Marcia too."

"We don't have all the answers right now. Hopefully, we'll be able to report back to you soon with more details. Will you stay at the hospital with your family for now?"

"Yes, I won't leave them. I refuse to."

"We'll be in touch soon. Take care, Kelvin."

"Just catch the bastards, Inspector."

Kelvin's words rattled around her mind as she and Dave raced through the hospital and out to the car. Dave drove while Kayli rang the station.

"Donna, it's me. The family are all okay. We're on our way back to the scene now to question the neighbours. We haven't delved into the neighbours' backgrounds yet, have we?"

"Can't do that without a name, boss. I can try just putting the address in to see what comes up, if you like. I've never tried that before."

"Try it, but don't waste much time on it. We'll gather some names and question the neighbours and then come back to base. I'm thinking along the lines that someone has a vendetta against the family. Kelvin was on night shift last night, but luckily, his boss sent him home early. I dread to think how far the fire would have spread if he hadn't been there. I'm pretty sure we would have been treating this as another murder enquiry if it wasn't for his quick thinking."

"Crap! That's all the family need, to be living in fear for the rest of their lives."

"Exactly. I refuse to let that happen. See you soon. Let me know if anything shows up on the system. Text me if you will, Donna."

"I'll do that, boss."

"Oh wait! One last thing. Do me a favour and chase up the sketch artist for me. We need to know who Samantha saw at the school and begin circulating her photo, now!"

Kayli ended the call and leaned back against the headrest. "Good call on the sketch artist. We could question the neighbours now and then return once we have the artist's drawing to hand to see if anyone saw the girl at the scene before the fire was started."

"Yeah, that was my thinking too."

Dave put his foot down and arrived in the Watsons' neighbourhood within twenty minutes. The area was still cordoned off, and a few of the neighbours were standing around, discussing the events of the morning. Kayli and Dave approached a group of four women, all of varying ages. Some were fully dressed, and a couple of them still wore their dressing gowns. One woman had a toddler on her hip. "Hello, everyone. I'm DI Kayli Bright, and this is my partner, DS Dave Chaplin. Mind if we have a chat with you all, separately?"

"Why? We didn't see anything. You can't stop us from looking as long as we remain behind the tape," the young woman holding the toddler said.

Kayli combatted the woman's off-hand statement with a smile. "We simply want to ask a few questions."

"There's no harm in that, Emma. Get off your high horse for a change," one of the older women said.

"You lot can do what you like. I'm having nothing to do with it. If the police had arrested the husband in the first place, I doubt this would have happened."

The hairs on the back of Kayli's neck stood on end. "You're giving me the impression that you think Kelvin Watson is guilty of killing his daughter Jamillia. Is that what you're implying?"

"Whatever," she snapped back, her lip curling up at the side.

"Dave, why don't you talk to these three ladies while I have a private chat with Emma? Sorry, I didn't catch your surname…"

"It's Emma Dawson," one of the other women shouted from the back of the group. "She always has a lot to say for herself."

"Up yours, Cindy."

"Shall we go inside and have a chat, Emma?" Kayli asked.

She sighed heavily and adjusted the little girl on her hip then led Kayli up the narrow path to a semi opposite the Watsons' smoking house.

"Let me put her in her playpen first."

"You do that."

Once the toddler was settled in the playpen in the kitchen, Emma motioned for Kayli to take a seat at the table.

Kayli sat down, her gaze fixed on the young woman as she dropped into the chair opposite her. "You seemed angry outside. May I ask why?"

"I have a right to be, knowing that there's a killer living on the estate."

Kayli frowned. "How do you know Mr. Watson is a murderer?"

"Bloody obvious from where I'm standing. You lot should have arrested him and taken him in for questioning."

"What makes you think that?"

"You can tell he's as guilty as sin. Shifty bugger, he is."

"He's never struck me as being that. Have you ever seen him ill-treat either of his children?"

Her eyes dropped to the table, and she shook her head. "No. That doesn't mean that he didn't abuse them, though."

"Granted. So, I have to ask, why the animosity towards him?"

The woman remained silent for a while.

Kayli pressed on. "Because he's black?"

Emma's head shot up, and her eyes bored into Kayli's. "I never said that."

"Then give me a suitable reason. Otherwise, I'll have no other option than to put this down as a racist POV."

"You can't say that. I'm not racist, not in the slightest."

"Then give me a good reason why you should suspect Mr. Watson of killing his own child."

She hitched up her shoulders. "I have a feeling, that's all. Usually, my gut feelings turn out to be correct."

"Give me some statistics?"

"What?"

Kayli sighed. "I need to verify how good your gut feelings are, so tell me how often you're right. A hundred percent of the time?"

"Nope. I'd say about ninety percent."

"Not bad. However, that still leaves ten percent ratio for error. Do you get where I'm going with this?"

Emma's eyes dropped to the table again, and a crimson colour filled her chubby cheeks. "Typical police. You always twist things when someone is trying to help you. You should look deeper into that man's past. That's all I'm saying."

Kayli tilted her head. "We have done that already and found nothing. Are you telling me that we've missed something?"

"That's all I'm saying. My boyfriend would be mad at me if he found out I'd grassed to the police."

"That's a mind-blowing statement you just made, Emma. Maybe I should ask you to get dressed and accompany me to the station."

"It ain't going to happen." She rose from her chair and walked to the door. "I'd like you to leave now. I need to get ready and go out for nappies for the baby."

"You haven't seen the last of me. Maybe I'll come back this evening when your boyfriend is at home."

"Do one. You come back then, and I'll deny ever speaking to you. Just do your job and dig into Watson's past. You'll be surprised what secrets you find lurking there."

"I will. Are you telling me that he's tried it on with you?"

"Nope. He wouldn't dare. I hear he likes them young, though," she replied with a tight smile.

"Okay. I'll keep digging. Here, should your conscience get the better of you and you decide to tell me what you know." Kayli handed her a card and walked out the front door, feeling frustrated beyond words. *Bitch! Maybe she's an attention seeker. We get them all the time. But then, I shouldn't discount what she says, either.*

Dave looked as dejected as she did when she joined him. "How did you get on?"

"As well as you, by the looks of things. Nothing."

"She's such a frustrating minx to deal with. I suspect she knows something. I just don't know how to get it out of her."

"Want me to have a word with her? Try the heavy-hand technique."

"No point. I already tried that." Kayli checked her emails to find one had arrived from Donna. She opened it to find an attachment with the picture the sketch artist had drawn of the young woman who had abducted Jamillia. "This might help. I'll send you a copy. Go back and ask the people you've just interviewed if they know the woman, and I'll do the same with the feisty Emma." She forwarded the message and returned to Emma's house. Kayli waited, tapping her foot, for the woman to answer the door. Eventually, Kayli lifted the flap on the letter box and shouted, "Emma, open the door please. It's Inspector Bright again."

She heard the woman reply, "I'm in the bathroom. You'll have to wait."

Kayli paced up and down the path for the next five minutes until

Emma, fully dressed, opened the door. "Sorry to disturb you again. I've just had a text and wanted to run something past you. Can I come in?"

"No. Just tell me what you want and then go."

Kayli's blood boiled in her veins. She opened her emails and showed the young, obstinate woman the drawing. She watched her expression very carefully and detected a faint recognition when Emma first laid eyes on the picture, then it quickly dissipated. "What's her name, Emma?"

"Haven't got a clue. I've never seen her before. Now if you'll excuse me, I have to get ready and go out."

"I know you're lying. If I find out you are, I'll be charging you with obstructing a police enquiry."

"Do what you like. I just want to keep out of this shit. Why don't you run along and do your job properly instead of sticking around here, pestering the neighbours?"

"You haven't heard the last of this, Emma. In the words of Schwarzenegger, 'I'll be back.'"

"Whatever. I've told you what I think you should do. I wish I'd kept my mouth shut now. I have no intention of helping you further."

"Why? What are you afraid of? *Who* are you afraid of?"

"Goodbye, Inspector."

Kayli turned and vented her frustration by kicking a stone lying in her way on the path. She met up with Dave back at the car. "Anything?"

Dave's mouth twisted. "Yes and no. One of them thought she'd seen the girl in the area, but couldn't give me a definite time or date when that was. How about you?"

"She recognised her, all right, but denied it outright. Something fishy is going on around here, Dave."

"With Watson?"

"Yep. How the hell we're going to find out what that is when no one is willing to help us, I have no friggin' idea. It's all very well people expecting the police to protect them, but if they're not willing to help us, what are we supposed to do?"

"I hope they bloody sleep well at night. That's all I have to say on the matter. Morons."

"We're done here. Let's grab some lunch on the way back."

"At the pub?" Dave asked, his eyes lighting up at the thought of a liquid lunch.

"Naughty. No, at the baker's on the high street."

"Worth a try."

## 11

Blackbird pulled up outside the cottage. A light was on in the kitchen, and the white van was in the drive. He was getting pretty fed up of coming out to the house every time one of them rang him with a query. He walked through the side gate and entered the kitchen. The pair of them were at it on the kitchen table. He slammed the door shut behind him, and they separated.

"Shit, man. You could've told us you were coming," Swift said angrily as he pulled up his trousers and tucked in his T-shirt.

Blackbird turned his back on the couple to let them finish getting dressed. "Arsehole, you knew what time I'd be here. If you can't control your urges, that's your lookout, not mine."

"Maybe you turned up early for the thrill factor of seeing us together," Magpie taunted, doing up her bra and taking her time to get dressed, unlike her partner.

"Like shit. I'll be glad when this job is over and we can go our separate ways. You two are annoying the shit out of me. Have you fed the girls today?" He turned to face the two youngsters who looked more embarrassed by his question than being caught humping.

"Yeah, of course," Magpie replied unconvincingly.

"Prove it." He walked over to the bin in the corner and rummaged around. He found nothing apart from the chip wrappers from the day before. "Liars. You want them dying on us because you couldn't be arsed to feed them? Then where will we be? Christ, I'm working with bloody amateurs."

Swift marched across the room and grabbed him round the throat. "I've had enough of you having a pop at us. You fuckin' stay here all day with them. I've had enough of this shit."

Blackbird wormed his way out of Swift's grasp and gasped for air. "Another week. That's all. If you can't hack it, fine. But if I have to replace you, you won't see a penny of the money due to us when we hand them over. It's your call, man."

Swift flung his arms out to the side. "I'm going stir-crazy here. It's not what I signed up for, and it's getting on my tits now."

"Fine. Go. Walk out the door, but say goodbye to any compensation you thought was coming your way."

Swift grabbed his crotch. "Suck my dick, arsehole."

"That's my job, sweetie. I don't like to share. You know that," Magpie said, sauntering up to Swift.

Blackbird tutted in disgust and flung himself into a chair at the table. "I didn't give up my lunchtime to come over here to witness you two screwing around. You called this meeting. Why?"

The two youngsters joined him at the table, one on either side of him.

Magpie smiled tentatively. "We've been talking. We need to replace the black girl."

"I came to the same conclusion. If your tosser of a boyfriend hadn't killed her, we wouldn't be in this mess. I'm expecting you to sort that out. How and when you do it is up to you. I want no part of it."

Swift glared at him and pointed. "I've got news for you, fucker. You're up to your neck in this shit whether you like it or not."

"Not for much longer. Do what you want. Just don't get caught."

"Where do we get another one? You're usually the one who tells us where and when," Magpie said, her lips pulling into a slight smile.

"Not my problem. I'm going down to see them. I suggest you start making them some sandwiches." He thrust his chair back and opened the door to the cellar. The body odour and smell of urine hit his nostrils on the way down the stairs. He had no idea what the couple upstairs expected from him, as they clearly weren't capable of looking after the children adequately. He would need to return later on that evening to ensure the kids were fed again.

The petrified girls cuddled together as he approached the cage. "Don't worry, little ones, lunch will be with you soon."

The three of them looked as though they needed a good soak in the bath, smelt like they could do with one, too. He should have felt some form of guilt for putting them in such a situation, but it was all about the money to him. *Why else would I be working with the idiots upstairs?*

He listened and could hear the couple messing around above him. They were truly beginning to get on his nerves. "All of this will be over soon enough. You'll get your freedom back next week." He smiled at the girls and took in their features one by one. None of the children reacted to his statement. "Don't you want to be free?"

When they still showed no reaction, he slammed his fist against the bars and bared his teeth in a sneer. "You should be nice to me. Show your appreciation more. Otherwise, things could turn out very differently. You know what happened to Jamillia." His smile pushed the sneer away. He saw tiny tears appear in the three girls' eyes at the mention of Jamillia.

Hearing footsteps behind him, he turned.

"Lunch as requested for the brats," Magpie stated, placing a plate piled high with scruffily made sandwiches on the chair beside the cage.

He nodded. "They'll need a drink. Get them one."

Retracing her steps up the stairs, Magpie chuntered under her breath. "Goddamn, I'm not your slave."

"No, but you were entrusted with their care," he called out after her.

She returned minutes later with a jug of water and some glasses. The tray rattled when she placed it on the floor next to the cage and left again before he could order her to do anything else.

He unhooked the key and unlocked the door. The girls tightened their hold on each other when he stepped through the door with the pile of sandwiches. They were frozen in time, scared to move, until he'd deposited the water and was back on the other side of the bars once again. He smiled. "Eat and drink, little ones. You'll need to keep your strength up for what lies ahead of you." His evil laugh made the girls flinch. He left them to it and returned upstairs.

"Satisfied?" Swift asked once the door to the cellar was shut and Blackbird had joined the other two at the table.

"For now. I need to ask you a question, and I expect an honest answer."

"Go on. We've got nothing to hide," Swift replied, gathering his girlfriend's hand in his.

"The Watsons' house has been all over the news today. Did you have anything to do with that?"

Magpie's hand covered her mouth, and she sniggered. "Stroke of genius, right?"

He shook his head in disgust. "Not. Why did you do it?"

"We needed to cause a distraction to the police. It was the only thing we could come up with. Great, right?"

"Bloody foolish if you ask me. I couldn't believe what I was hearing on the way into work this morning. If anything, you've led the police to think this is some kind of vendetta against the parents, instead of Watson torching his own home. How the hell is that going to be a distraction to the police?"

Magpie fell silent, and Swift glared at him. "You think you're so fuckin' smart and that you have all the damn answers, don't ya?"

"Let's put it this way: I'm a darn sight smarter than the pair of you put together. That much is bloody evident. Now you're talking about picking up another girl. I hope, for your sake, you plan out the abduction properly before attempting it. I'm out of here. I'll drop by this evening if I have time."

"You'll turn up whether you have the time or not. We've got a date this evening that we plan on keeping. Tickets to a concert." Blackbird glared at him. "Don't look at me like that. I booked them months ago, before we started this gig. You can sit here, keeping an eye on the kids for a change. It won't hurt you to do your share. You've got off light so far."

"And what if I can't make it?"

Swift shrugged. "Ain't our problem if you want to leave the kids alone for a few hours. I ain't ferrying any guilt to the concert with us."

"I'll be here." He rose from his chair. "Watch what you're doing and stop antagonising the police. They're smarter than you think, especially the inspector in charge."

"You worry too much, man. Leave it to us. Be here at six. We need to leave by six fifteen." Swift reached for Magpie's hand and thrust it in the air. "In the meantime, we'll snatch another kid this afternoon. We're the A-Team, so you'll need to feed an extra mouth tonight."

Blackbird shook his head and left the cottage, mixed feelings running through him. Annoyance and anger the most prevalent ones. The last thing he wanted or needed after a long day at work was to spend hours sitting in the cottage, alone.

*Except you won't be alone.* The girls, all four of them by then, would be there to keep him company. He smiled. *Maybe it won't be such a bad night after all!*

## 12

Donna and Graeme were both busy at their computers when Kayli and Dave walked into the incident room. "How are things going? Did you manage to circulate the artist's drawing, Donna?"

"I did, boss. Not had any response from anyone as yet. I'm going through the database, trying to find a possible match, but nothing has jumped out at me there, either."

"Damn. We could sure do with a break on this case. Keep trying." Kayli grabbed a coffee and walked into her office. She dropped into her chair. After eating the sandwich they'd stopped off to buy, she got to work on the one chore aggravating her more than the lack of progress with the case: her paperwork, and she whisked through the brown envelopes in her in-tray, determined to get the job finished in record time.

Halfway through the afternoon, her phone rang. It was the control centre. "Hello, DI Bright. I know you're dealing with the child murder in the area. I thought this would be of interest to you."

"Go on, I'm all ears."

"We're getting reports of a little girl being abducted from a children's swing park, not far from the school where Jamillia Watson attended."

"Give me the details." She unhooked her coat from the back of the chair and shouted for Dave to join her.

He appeared in the doorway, a frown pulling at his forehead. "Boss?"

"Get ready to head out. We've got a child abduction case just being reported. I'm getting the details now."

"Shit! Okay, I'm ready to go when you are." He left the room.

The officer gave Kayli the location and wished her luck, then she ended the call.

"Damn, here we go again. Graeme, I'm not sure of the area where the park is. It's Cornwall Crescent. Find out what CCTV is in operation in that area and get me the footage ASAP. Let's strike quickly with this one, okay?"

"Yes, boss." He picked up his phone and punched in a number.

Kayli and Dave rushed down the stairs and got in Dave's car, as he insisted that he should drive.

Her pulse rate escalated the closer they got to the scene. "Why? Bloody hell, in broad daylight too. What is wrong with these people? It's as if they enjoy taking risks."

"Or take pleasure in winding us up," Dave added glumly.

"Either way, I'd say they're going to chance their arm too often, and hopefully, that will be their undoing. Broad bloody daylight! That's unheard of, right?"

"Not come across anything like it before, boss. Do we know how old the child is? Dare I ask even, because I'm guessing it's below school age, given the time of day?"

"Yep, you'd be right. She's three."

Dave struck the steering wheel several times. Each hit was accompanied by a different expletive.

Kayli rubbed his arm to comfort him. "I feel the same way, mate. Something needs to start going our way in this case and soon. Who knows how many frigging kids they're going to abduct if we don't catch the bastards."

"We need to get every officer in this city watching out for these guys. That's the only way we're going to catch them."

"And tell them what? To be on the lookout for a white van? It would be different if we had a registration number, but we haven't."

"We do have something in our favour: the abductor's picture. Maybe it's time we called on the media and started using them to circulate it for us? Someone in this city must have a name for her."

"You read my mind. I was hoping to hold that card up my sleeve for a while, until Donna had completed her search of the database, but these guys have just forced our hand. I thought if we mentioned it through the media too soon that she and her accomplice, either singular or plural, would go underground, but needs must now. That's assuming she's working alongside someone. That's another thing we're unsure about."

"She has to be. Samantha said she thrust Jamillia in a van and barely closed the door before it took off. She had to have a getaway driver ready and waiting for her."

Kayli tutted. "You're right, I'd forgotten all about that. Still, I'm not getting the feeling that we're closing in on these tyrants yet. Let's hope something good comes of the CCTV footage, if there is any."

Dave parked the car in the first available slot, and they ran across the road and into the park. The area had been cordoned off already. Kayli flashed her warrant card and dipped under the tape. At the far end, past all the swings, slides and roundabouts, were two women and a child. One of the women, a petite blonde, was crying and shouting at the uniformed female officer talking to her. The officer looked in their direction. She excused herself from the frantic woman and walked towards them.

"What have we got, PC Vincent?"

The officer pointed over her shoulder with her pen in the mother's direction. "The two women were talking while the kids played on the equipment. The brunette, whose daughter is safe, told me that they presumed the kids were playing together, but when little Jenny came running back without Belinda Wainwright, the women started to panic. They were searching the area high and low, thinking Belinda was playing hide-and-seek, when Jenny said that a nice lady gave Belinda a teddy bear to play with. That's when the penny dropped and panic set in. The mother called 999 right away."

"Thanks. We'll have a quick word with them now." Kayli smiled as she closed the gap between them. "I'm so sorry this has happened. Constable Vincent has filled me in. Did you see anyone hanging around the park before your daughter was taken, Mrs. Wainwright?"

"It's miss. Please, you have to find her. She's all I've got."

Kayli smiled at the other woman. "Did you notice anyone?"

She was holding her daughter tightly and shook her head. "No, we didn't see anyone."

"We shouldn't have been talking. We should have been keeping an eye on our daughters. It's the first time we've had to ourselves for weeks, and... this happened. Please bring my daughter back to me. I'm begging you. She's only three. Oh God, I can't bear to think of what that person will do to her." She started to sob uncontrollably. Her friend slung an arm around her shoulder, but she shrugged it off.

"Can we give you a lift home, Miss Wainwright?" Kayli said, unsure what else she could say to put the woman's mind at rest.

Dave coughed to gain Kayli's attention. "Boss, do you want me to start knocking on the doors, see if any of the homeowners saw anything?"

"Yes, you do that. Do something, for Christ's sake," Miss Wainwright said, drying her eyes with a tissue.

"Thanks, Dave. I'll stay here. Report back to me the minute you hear anything useful."

Kayli watched her partner rush across the street to the houses opposite. "We've got an alert out for your daughter. I know it's easier said than done, but please try and remain calm. I'm sure we'll get your daughter back to you quickly."

"How? Do you know who has taken her?"

Miss Wainwright's friend, who informed them she was called Sandy Thomas, frowned. "Hey, aren't you the one dealing with that murder case? I saw your picture on TV, on the news, didn't I?"

"Yes. That's right. I'm not saying the two cases are connected, but it's also not something we're willing to rule out at this point."

"Murder case... nooo!" Miss Wainwright howled before she collapsed to the ground.

Kayli swept down to see if the woman was okay. She was out cold. "Ring for an ambulance," she ordered PC Vincent, who immediately actioned the request on her radio.

"They're on their way."

In the distance, Kayli saw Dave run across the road and gather speed as he came towards them. "It was the white van. The old man was looking out the window. I showed him the picture of the suspect, and he can't be sure, but he thinks she was the one who led the little girl away and put her in the van. The van left soon after. I asked him if it drove away fast. He said no, at normal speed. Nice and casual."

"Excuse me," Sandy interrupted. "Are you saying you know who has Belinda?"

Kayli motioned for the officer to take care of the woman lying on the ground and stood up. "We believe so. Another witness worked with a sketch artist. She told us that a woman showed up at a school to pick up one of the pupils. Unfortunately, we've yet to identify the woman."

"That's not right, surely. How or why would a woman be involved in this?" the lady asked.

Kayli shook her head. "It's still a mystery to us."

Sirens wailed in the adjoining street and it wasn't long before an ambulance pulled up at the gates to the park. Two paramedics, a male and a female, rushed towards them.

Constable Vincent filled the crew in while Kayli took down the woman's particulars. "I'll need Miss Wainwright's address too. Do you know if she has any next of kin we can contact?"

Sandy was unsure if Miss Wainwright had any family living locally or not.

"Not to worry. Constable Vincent, are you free to go to the hospital with the ladies?"

Sandy shook her head. "I can't go to the hospital. I hate to run out on her in her time of need, but I have to pick up my boy from school. He's due out in twenty minutes. I'm sorry."

"No problem. I can go with Miss Wainwright, ma'am. It would be my pleasure," PC Vincent said with a smile.

Kayli handed Sandy a business card then nodded appreciatively at the constable and asked, "Keep me informed of Miss Wainwright's progress, will you?"

"I will, ma'am," PC Vincent said.

"We're going to head back to the station to get things rolling. My team are already looking into the CCTV footage in this area. We'll do our best to find Belinda, I promise."

Sandy nodded. "I'm sure Rachel will be relieved to hear that. Please find her, for Rachel's sake. She's had a shit year so far what with her boyfriend running out on her after he cheated with her best friend. Men! They really are the pits."

"Do you know the boyfriend's name?"

"Adam Cosgrove. Not sure of his address, though."

"I hate to ask, but I'm presuming Rachel will have his phone number in her phone. Would you mind taking a look for me?"

"Good idea. He should know about this… Oh my God, you don't think he's behind this, do you?"

"I doubt it, but he has a right to know that his daughter has been abducted. It wouldn't be right of me to keep this from him."

Sandy looked in Rachel's handbag and fished out her mobile. "Damn, I have no idea of her password. I can't help you, sorry."

Rachel stirred and sat up. She stared at them, her brow wrinkled with puzzlement. "What's going on? Oh no, I remember. Have you found her yet?"

"No. Look, the paramedics are going to take you to hospital to check you over. We were just trying to find your ex-boyfriend's number, but your phone is locked."

"Why? He wouldn't do this. He might be the biggest shit to ever walk this earth, but he'd never sink that low."

"I'm not suggesting he would, but we'll need to make him aware of the situation all the same." Sandy passed the mobile to Rachel, and she entered her password and located her ex's number. Then she handed the phone to Kayli to note it down. "That's brilliant. You take care, and I'll be in touch soon. Sandy has given me all your details. The quicker we get on with the investigation, the sooner we'll bring your daughter back to you."

"Thank you. Do your best, Inspector. She's all I have."

"Do you have a picture of your daughter with you?"

Rachel delved through her large handbag and withdrew a slightly crumpled photo of an angelic blonde child. Kayli's heart sank. For the first time in ages, hopelessness prodded her all over.

Kayli and Dave walked away from the group and took a moment to gather their thoughts by the railings surrounding the play area.

"Let's hope we get something on the CCTV footage. This girl is getting brazen, snatching a kid in broad daylight—a young one, at that. Damn, a bloody three-year-old!" Her hand swept a stray long hair behind her ear.

"Don't. It doesn't bear thinking about. I think you need to get onto the media quickly about this."

"That's my intention. First I need to ring the girl's father." Kayli punched in the number Rachel had given her and tapped her foot while she waited for the call to be answered.

A man's abrupt voice answered the phone.

"Hello, Mr. Adam Cosgrove?"

"Yes. Who wants to know?" he said tersely.

"I'm DI Kayli Bright from the Avon and Somerset Constabulary, sir. May I ask where you are?"

"At work. What's this about, Inspector?"

"If it's all right with you, sir, I'd rather tell you that in person. What's the address?"

"Now you're scaring the life out of me. Please, just tell me."

"Very well. I'm standing in the play area on Cornwall Crescent..."

"I know the place. My ex usually takes my daughter there. What about it?"

"Sir, it's about your daughter. I'm sorry to inform you that she's gone missing."

"What? How? Missing? Wasn't Rachel with her? How can she go missing?"

"Sorry, not missing exactly. Belinda has been abducted."

"Jesus Christ! What… I'm coming over there. Is her mother there? Put her on the damn phone."

"Please, sir. I'm going to have to ask you to calm down. Yes, Rachel is here. Paramedics are with her at present. They're just preparing to take her to the hospital."

"What? Is she injured? Just give me the facts, Inspector, for Christ's sake!"

"Rachel fainted. Look, I need to get on with the investigation. I just wanted to fill you in on what had occurred before I ask the media for their help."

"I understand. I'm leaving work now. I'll go to the hospital to see Rachel and go from there. Please do everything you can to get my daughter back, Inspector. I can't believe this nightmare is happening to us. Why take a three-year-old? Do you know who took her?"

"We have a witness who saw what happened and has given us a statement. We need to press on and deal with the information the witness gave us. I have to ask, Mr. Cosgrove, is there anyone you can think of who might have taken your daughter?"

"What? Are you crazy? You think I hang around with child abductors? That's absurd!"

"No, not in the slightest. I had to ask, sorry. I'll be in touch soon." Kayli ended the call and sighed. "God, I hate making calls like that. Much prefer to break bad news face to face. He's going to the hospital to be with Rachel, but I'm not about to tell her that. Come on, Dave, we need to get back to the station."

They rushed back to the car and flicked on the siren to aid their swift return to base.

The rest of the afternoon flew by. Kayli managed to get a few of the more influential media folk in the area gathered within a few hours. She spoke to members of the TV and newspaper media. They were all appalled by what she divulged, and they promised to get the information out there ASAP. In the conference, she revealed not only Belinda

Wainwright's identity, but also the sketch artist's drawing of the possible abductor.

The waiting game had begun, again. It was gone eight thirty when she finally left work that evening. Her team had offered to stay at the station with her, but she'd insisted they leave hours ago. She was determined to man the phone herself, in the hope that someone might have spotted the mystery woman in the drawing, but no such information came her way.

~

*B*lackbird arrived at the cottage around five thirty. He picked up the latest Ian Rankin book from the passenger seat, together with the bag with four portions of chips and several pieces of cod, then locked the car door. He heard the laughter of his two partners in crime as he rounded the side of the house and walked through the back door.

The couple had their lips locked in a heated kiss when he opened the door and walked in. "Save it till later, guys. Are you off now?"

"You're only jealous, lonely old man!" Swift goaded him.

He shrugged and placed the items on the table. "I take it the kids haven't eaten."

"That's right. You're on babysitting duties tonight. That task is down to you. We're off. Don't wait up. We could be late."

"Hey, not too late. I have to get up early for work. Ten o'clock at the latest—you hear me?"

Swift crossed the room quickly and stood in front of him, a menacing stance that caused him to shrink back a little. "The night is about to get going at ten, man. If you need to leave, then shut the door behind you and place the key under the pot outside the back door. It's that simple."

"I have no intention of leaving the kids here alone. That would be dumb."

"Whatever, man. I'm past caring. The sooner I get my life back, the better. If you go down there, you'll find an added bonus."

Blackbird's eyes widened. "You've picked up another kid?"

Swift laughed. "You'll see. Hey, their dinner is getting cold. We're off duty now. See ya later—or not, as the case may be."

He watched the two of them leave, hands all over each other and roaring with laughter. He listened for the van to pull away before he filled three glasses with water and hooked the carrier bag containing the food over his wrist. He walked down the staircase once his eyes had adjusted to the dark. Though Blackbird doubted the veracity of Swift's plan, it had been agreed that the light should remain off at all times and the bulb had been taken out, to make it more difficult for the kids to recognise them.

He heard subtle sobbing as he approached the cage. The three girls were huddled together, and in the middle was something that caused him to stand still and shake his head as his mouth dropped open. Placing the glasses of water on the uneven floor, he rubbed his eyes, unsure if what he was seeing was correct. "Shit!" he uttered, his anger mounting and making his blood course through his veins like molten lava.

The tiny girl was sobbing and shielding her face in the chest of the girl to her right. *What the hell have they done? She's far too young. She must only be about three, for fuck's sake!*

"Sshh... little one. I won't hurt you." He unhooked the key and opened the door after which he deposited the bag of food. None of the girls moved towards the food, which was unusual for them. Keeping one eye on the group, he dipped back outside the cage to collect the glasses of water. He was one short, and there were no more upstairs. "You'll have to share these."

None of the girls responded. He stared at the youngest member of the group, appalled and ashamed to be involved in her abduction. *This had nothing to do with me. Those morons did this—not me. The bastards. They knew how I would react once I saw how young she was. What the fuck am I doing in business with these idiots?*

At a loss for what to say and do next, he backed out of the cage and returned upstairs. His appetite diminished, he turned on the TV screen and switched to the local news. Staring back at him was a sketch of

Magpie, alongside a photograph of the little mite he'd seen in the cellar. He paced the floor for hours, formulating a plan. *I'll make them regret taking me for a damn fool.*

It turned out to be a torturously long evening. Although he used the time to pull a plan together, he also found himself getting more wound up about his cohorts' stupidity. He watched the hands on his watch slowly tick over, every minute seemingly stretched longer than the last until twelve fifty arrived and he heard the van pull up outside. The youngsters were noisy in their approach to the cottage. Out in the sticks, they knew they wouldn't disturb anyone anyway. Both of them sounded drunk, which tipped his mood over the edge, and he let them have it as soon as they entered the back door.

"What the fuck are you two playing at? Drinking and driving? Are you bloody crazy? Do you want to get caught?"

Swift staggered towards him and poked him in the chest. Slurring his words badly, he replied, "Who the fuck do ya think you are? My mother?"

Magpie sniggered, finding the situation amusing rather than dangerous.

Blackbird shoved Swift away from him. "You make me sick. Between the two of you, you've managed to screw everything up." Pointing at Magpie, he added, "Are you aware your picture was all over the news tonight?"

Her eyes widened, and her smile vanished. She dropped into one of the chairs around the table. "What? Is this some kind of joke?"

"I wish it fucking was. What were you thinking taking a bloody three-year-old, for fuck's sake? Someone must have seen you. The picture was drawn by a sketch artist and on the screen alongside a picture of the girl."

"Shit!" the youngsters said in unison.

"Help us get out of this fix." Magpie continued.

Blackbird placed a hand over his chest. "Me? You want my help? It's a pity you didn't run the idea past me in the first bloody place. A three-year-old! What the hell were you thinking? My best guess tells me that you weren't thinking, not in the slightest. I've had it with you two." He flung his arms out to the side, grabbed his keys off the table, and rushed towards the door.

A staggering Swift tried to stand in his way. Blackbird shoved him aside. The drunken man dramatically lost his balance as if he were an elephant on ice skates and ended up in a heap on the floor. "Either you two get your frigging act together, or I'm calling the whole thing off and getting rid of the girls."

Swift tried desperately to stand up, but the way his eyes moved in his head, Blackbird could tell he was dizzy. "You can't do that! We got a deal."

"We *had* a deal. Until you fuckwits decided to branch out into taking kids barely out of their nappies. I'm done with you. I'm out of here."

"You can't leave us like this," Magpie insisted. She ran at him unsteadily in her heels and grasped the front of his jacket. "Please, please give us one last chance."

"Why should I? You don't listen to me. You're a couple of know-it-alls, when it's clear you know fuck all. Get out of my face. Sleep it off. I'll be back tomorrow for the final time. Think on what I've said, and we'll discuss what you're going to do with the new girl upon my return."

From his position on the floor, Swift shouted, "You ain't the boss around here. We're equals in this, and that kid ain't going anywhere."

"Shut up!" Magpie replied, striking him across the face. "Just shut the fuck up!"

Blackbird gave a final shrug then left the cottage. He eased around the side of the building, fearful that the cops might have followed the van to their hideaway, but the coast was clear. On the drive home, he cursed himself for not taking the opportunity of dobbing the youngsters in to the police while they were out. Now he would have to think of another way of getting his own back on them. If they refused to get rid of the new girl, maybe he should suggest he do it instead. That way, he would be assured the job was dealt with properly.

His distrust of the others grew every time they did something wrong. He wanted to end his partnership with them and quickly.

## 13

The rain was non-stop, and Kayli's windscreen wipers worked constantly on her way into work. Kayli dashed across the car park, towards the building. Her mobile rang just as she yanked open the door to the front entrance. "Hello. Kayli Bright."

"Morning, it's Naomi. Hope you're not driving?"

"Morning, Naomi. No, I've just arrived at work. What have you got for me?"

Naomi let out a long sigh. "Sorry to drop this on you first thing, but I'm at another murder scene."

"Don't tell me, the victim is another child."

"You guessed right. She was found in a disused warehouse on the old industrial estate on the edge of town."

"The Hawksby Estate?"

"That's the one. Do you want to join me? My team have been here all night. I arrived at six this morning, and I'm about ready to pack up and leave. I'll stick around and walk you through the scene if you can be here within twenty minutes."

"On my way now. I've just spotted Dave arriving. Depends on the traffic at this time of the morning whether we make it in time. Any chance you can extend that twenty minutes?"

"As it's you, okay. Make it snappy, though."

Naomi hung up, and Kayli rushed out the building and pointed at her car as Dave swiftly moved towards her. "Get in. Don't ask. I'll fill you in on the way."

"Good morning to you too, boss. Nice weather, if you've got feathers."

"Ha! Morning, Dave, and sorry." She unlocked the car, and once they were both inside and the car was pulling out of the car park, she recapped her conversation with Naomi.

Dave's face was etched with fury, and he lashed out at the dashboard. "Fuck! What the heck is going on? Do we know the victim's identity yet?"

"No, not yet. That's all we've got for now. Naomi was in a bit of a rush to finish up."

"Why abduct the kids if all they're going to do is kill them, er… you know what I mean. It doesn't make sense."

"The girls outlive their usefulness after a while. I'd rather not say what images that builds up in my head, but at this stage, that's all that comes to mind. Let's not get ahead of ourselves. Naomi didn't mention any similarities to Jamillia's case, so let's leave the speculation until we get there. It's sickening, either way. If the crimes are linked, then I'm getting the impression that the criminals are frigging laughing at us. We need to find that woman and the van, pronto. Call Donna for me, explain where we're going, and see if there have been any leads overnight from the media coverage."

Dave fished his phone out of his pocket and rang the station. "Donna, it's Dave. We're en route to another crime scene. The boss told me to ring you, to see if anything surfaced overnight from the appeal."

Half-listening to her partner's conversation, Kayli weaved through the mounting traffic until it became gridlocked. Dave prodded her leg and circled his finger in the air. Kayli flicked the switch to initiate the siren. A few of the cars in front squeezed forward a little, but until the lights changed up ahead, there was little Kayli could do to rectify their imprisonment.

Dave ended the call. "Okay, there's been a very disappointing response so far. Let's hope people have had the chance to think about the images overnight and they start ringing in later. I was thinking about the case last night, and you know what we haven't done yet?"

"No, go on."

"Shown the sketch to Kelvin Watson."

Kayli's eyes narrowed. "That's right. The neighbour opposite showed a glimmer of recognition. We definitely need to run it past him. Let's deal with this new scene first and then shoot over there to see him."

Dave gave her a smug smile. "Makes sense to me."

"All right, don't rub it in, Dave. It's not as if we've been sat on our arses not doing anything, is it?"

"Granted. Take a left here; it's a shortcut."

"Really? I hope it's not one that will lead us to a dead end. I remember the last shortcut you told me to take when we were in a hurry. We nearly ended up in the dock, right?"

"Oh, yeah. Okay, maybe don't take this route then."

Kayli let out an exasperated breath and took the shortcut anyway. It turned out to be a wise move as it led them directly to the location within a few minutes. They rushed out of the car and through the jagged opening in the side of the dilapidated building.

Naomi was instructing her team and glanced up when they approached.

"Sorry for the delay, bloody traffic was chocka. What are we looking at, Naomi? Same MO? Any ID yet?" Kayli said breathlessly.

"I'll show you." She took them across the rubble-strewn area and stopped alongside a shape that had been covered with a sheet.

Kayli braced herself for the unveiling and felt Dave tense beside her. Naomi removed the sheet. Kayli's eyes widened, and she heard Dave gulp noisily.

"Fuck! Why?" Dave muttered.

"Stand over there if it's too much, Dave. I can handle it, I think." Kayli was trying to protect him, but in doing so, was putting all the onus on herself to deal with the atrocity. The child was covered in bruises, and there was a thick rope around her neck. She looked above her head and then over at Naomi, who was nodding.

"Yes, she was hanging from the beam when we got here."

Tears misted her eyes. "Who found her? Do we know?"

Naomi pointed to an elderly man sitting on a large pile of rubble behind her. "He did. He was walking his dog last night, and the dog came into the building and started barking. I take it you didn't get a call then?"

"Obviously. Otherwise, I would have attended the scene at the time. Why is he still here?"

"I've tried to persuade him to go home, but he's saying that his legs are refusing to work, and he wants to stay here with the child."

"What? How strange. I need to have a word with him."

Naomi caught her arm. "Let me finish telling you what I've discovered before you rush off. I need to get going."

"Sorry, I'm all ears, hon. Dave, go and have a word with the old man, see if he needs any assistance, an ambulance or something."

Dave nodded and set off. Naomi shouted after him, "I've already asked."

"Sorry, I wasn't suggesting you hadn't, of course you would have. Bloody hell, Naomi, who could do this? Do you think it's connected to the Watson case?"

"My instinct is telling me yes. My team are continuing to hunt for some form of DNA, but it could take them days to come up with anything."

Kayli glanced down at the child's naked body again. "Evidence of intercourse?"

"Upon first glance, yes. I'll know more later. That was sitting alongside the body."

Kayli followed Naomi's pointed finger to the evidence bag containing a thick stick. "Bloody unthinkable!" Kayli shook her head in disgust. "How long has she likely been here? Any idea?"

"Maybe a day or two. Hard to give a definite estimation, sorry. Look, I've got to get going. I wanted you to see the scene for yourself. Sorry, you're going to have to clear up the mess and break the news to yet another traumatised family. Let me know if I can help. I'll send you the results of the PM in the next day or so. Good luck—you're going to bloody need it with this one."

"Thanks, Naomi. I'll snag a photo with my phone and try to find a match with the missing persons database when we return to the station. I need to help this old-timer get home first."

As Naomi left, Kayli walked towards the old man. Dave was on his haunches alongside him, petting the man's dog, who was lying patiently beside his master. "Hello, sir. I'm very sorry that you've had to witness this dreadful incident, but we truly appreciate you placing the call."

He glanced up at her and scrubbed at his colourless cheek. "I couldn't leave her here alone, still can't leave her. I feel responsible in some way, daft as it may seem. Maybe if I'd taken Lucky out for his walk an hour or so earlier, I could have prevented her death."

Kayli bent down and touched his hand. "Sir, that wouldn't have happened. The pathologist believes the little girl died possibly twenty-four to forty-eight hours ago." She straightened up and smiled. "Come on, let's take you home. There's nothing more either of us can do here."

Kayli motioned for Dave to join her, and between them, they raised the man to his feet. Lucky stood up too and followed them to the car. Kayli opened the back door and helped Dave ease the man into the backseat. His dog jumped onto the seat beside him.

"Is Lucky all right sitting on your seat? I haven't got his blanket with me."

"Yes, he's fine. Where are we going, sir?"

"Can you drop me at my sister's place? Not sure I could face going home to dwell on things in an empty house."

"Sure. What's the address?"

Fortunately, Dave knew the location when the man reeled off the address. It was within a five-minute drive of their location. When they arrived, Dave helped the man from the vehicle and walked him up the path to the quaint cottage. An old lady opened the door and immediately covered her mouth with her hand. Then Dave disappeared into the house for a few minutes before he returned to the car.

"He'll be fine. He's shook up, but his sister promised to look after him."

"Good, let's go."

When they arrived at the station, Dave headed back to the incident room, and Kayli made her way to the Missing Persons Department.

"Hi, Barb. It's me again. I've just been at the scene of yet another child's murder. The thing is, I don't recognise the girl from the photos we looked through the last time we searched the database. Maybe I'm wrong, though." Kayli showed the woman the picture of the girl on her phone.

Barbara flinched and gasped. "Poor child. Let's see what we can find. Maybe we should extend the search area, see if she shows up then?"

Kayli pulled up a chair and nodded. "Sounds like a good idea to me. Sorry for shocking you like that. I didn't really think."

"You might be used to seeing dead bodies every day. That happens to be my first one, of a child anyway. Makes me sick to the stomach. Callous shits whoever did this to her."

"Agreed. We really haven't got any further with the other case we're working on, but looks like this one might be connected. We won't know more until the result of the PM comes in."

Barbara hit a few keys on her keyboard, and the search began. It took thirty minutes for them to find a possible match.

"I'm not sure, are you?" Kayli asked, trying to visualise the girl's face without the coloured patches of bruising.

"I'm pretty sure that's her. If there was any doubt, I would have continued with the search."

"Okay, can you print it off for me? I want to look at it from a different angle."

The printer spewed out the single sheet of paper. Barbara fetched it and handed it to Kayli. Together they analysed the pictures, turning them at different angles, before the pair of them were satisfied they had found the right girl.

Barbara then pulled up the girl's file and wrote down her address and phone number, plus the details of the officer in charge of the case. Armed with the information, Kayli thanked Barbara for her help and ran up the flight of stairs to the incident room. "I've got her ID. Sophie Hall. Graeme, will you add her name and that of Belinda Wainwright to the whiteboard, please?"

Graeme's chair screeched on the floor as he stood up. "Will do, boss."

"I need a coffee, then I'm going to ring the detective dealing with Sophie's case."

Kayli took her cup into the office, let out a large breath, and dialled the detective's number. "Detective Lomas, this is DI Kayli Bright of the Avon and Somerset Constabulary."

"Hello, ma'am. What can I do for you?"

"You're dealing with a missing persons case, I believe. Sophie Hall."

"That's right. Don't tell me you've found her?"

"Unfortunately, yes. A member of the public found her hanging in a warehouse. I don't wish to step on your toes, but I'd like to inform the parents myself, as well as interview them. I'm investigating another child murder on my patch and think the two crimes might be connected."

"Damn, I had a feeling this would be the outcome. Be my guest. I'd be lost as to what to say to them anyway."

"I appreciate that, thanks." Kayli ended the call and walked around the room to compose herself for the second call she had to make. She detested having to deliver bad news—every serving officer did—but it was part of the job. Picking up the phone, she punched in the numbers slowly. A woman's faint voice answered after the third ring.

"Hello, is that Mrs. Hall?"

"It is."

"This is DI Kayli Bright from the Avon and Somerset Constabulary."

The woman gasped. "Have you found my Sophie?"

"I'd like to come and see you if that's possible. Are you free now?"

"Yes. Please, just tell me. Have you found her?"

Kayli sighed heavily. "Can you arrange for your husband to be there too?"

"You have found her, haven't you? Please, don't make me wait. I have to know."

"I'm sorry. The last thing I want to do is build your hopes up. I'd rather not say this over the phone but… it's not good news. I could be there in half an hour."

The woman screamed. Kayli held the phone away from her ear, but it was too late. She suspected she'd already suffered slight damage to her eardrum, but it was nothing compared to what Mrs. Hall was about to go through.

The phone clattered onto a piece of furniture, and she heard Mrs. Hall sobbing on the other end. Kayli hung up and rushed through the incident room. "Dave, with me, quickly."

## 14

The Halls' home was a semi-detached house on the outskirts of a small Devonshire village just over the border. Kayli rang the bell and swallowed hard. Dave also swallowed noisily as he stood alongside her.

A man in his early thirties opened the door. His eyes were red, evidence that he'd been crying.

"Hello, Mr. Hall. I'm DI Bright, and this is my partner, DS Chaplin."

"You better come in. My wife is in the lounge, first on the left."

Kayli smiled at the man and walked past him and into the lounge. Mrs. Hall was sitting on the couch, a large black flat-coated retriever lying on the floor by her feet. The dog remained seated but looked in their direction when they entered the room.

"Hello, Mrs. Hall. We spoke earlier."

"Yes. Take a seat."

Kayli and Dave sat down in the two easy chairs on one side of the room while Mr. Hall sat on the couch close to his wife. He gripped her hand in his.

"I really didn't want to break the news over the phone like that. I would have rather done it in person."

"I know I pushed you. I regret doing that now. Thank you for coming to see us so soon," Mrs. Hall replied with a sniffle.

"How did it happen?" Mr. Hall demanded.

"A man walking his dog found your daughter's body in a warehouse in Bristol."

His hand swept over his face as the couple glanced at each other. "What? Why there?"

"We've yet to establish any facts regarding the case. What I can tell you is that we believe your daughter's case is linked with another murder we've been dealing with for the past few weeks."

"Are you telling us that you have a suspect in mind?"

"Not at this moment. We're still conducting enquiries and gathering evidence."

"That statement doesn't exactly fill me with confidence, Inspector."

"I'm sorry, Mr. Hall. Can you tell me about your daughter's disappearance?"

At that moment, the dog's head lifted at the sound of a child crying.

"I need to go. Billy needs me." Mrs. Hall got to her feet, and the dog followed her out of the room.

"We have a two-year-old son, who has been missing his sister. How the hell are we going to tell him that he'll never see her again?" He swiped away a tear as it seeped onto his cheek.

"I'm so sorry. I just don't know what to say to that."

"It was a rhetorical question, Inspector."

"I know." Kayli heaved out a huge sigh. "I'm so very sorry. I know my timing could be better, but I need to ask you some questions."

"If it'll help capture the twisted shit who killed my daughter, then fire away. I'll do what I can to answer. You asked how Sophie disappeared. Well, she was coming home from school. Our friend said that she would pick her up as I was on an airport run. I'm a cab driver. Sharon had an appointment at the doctors' with the little one."

"I see. Did your friend forget to pick her up?"

"No, she picked her up and took her back to her house, which is just around the corner. Sophie wanted to come home early. Claire told her she had to wait until I collected her, but when Claire was distracted, Sophie opened the front door and walked out. Claire was frantic when she realised what had happened. She was in the garden getting the washing in at the time. It wasn't her fault; Sophie wasn't the most patient child." His head dipped, admonishing himself for speaking disrespectfully about his eldest child.

"It's okay. These things happen when you have children. It's impossible to watch their every move twenty-four hours a day."

He lifted his head and wiped the tears on his sleeve. "I know, which is what I told Claire and Sharon. Anyway, we searched the streets for her for four hours solid. A few of my cabbie mates even lent a hand, but she'd vanished into thin air."

"Just covering all angles here. Has anyone contacted you with a ransom demand?"

"No. We haven't heard anything until you rang my wife. The detective dealing with the case said he would keep us informed. I rang him every few days—she's been missing four weeks now—and I received the same reply. Nothing. No contact. No clues. Absolutely nothing at all."

"I'm sure he was doing his very best, and I can understand the detective's frustrations. I spoke to him earlier. He was very upset to learn that Sophie's body had been found."

"I don't blame him. Like I said, she just vanished. I don't see what, if anything, could have been done differently. Maybe if a witness had come forward to say they had seen her being abducted… but they didn't. My colleagues are still keeping their eyes open for her. They'll be as devastated as we are to hear the news that she won't be coming home."

"Did you see the news on TV last night, Mr. Hall?"

"No. Did it mention you finding Sophie's body?" he asked, frowning.

Kayli took out her phone. "No. I instructed the media to put out a call for help in locating a three-year-old girl and the person we believe abducted her yesterday. I wondered if you knew this young woman." She walked across the room and handed him her phone. He stared at the image then looked up at her with his mouth gaping and his eyes wide open. Kayli's heart skipped several beats then hammered against her ribs. "Do you know this woman?"

He pushed her aside as he rushed towards the door. "Sharon... Sharon, get down here, now!"

Kayli stared at Dave. "Sir, do you know this girl?" Dave repeated Kayli's question.

"I need to clarify it with Sharon first. I think so."

His wife came thundering down the stairs, cradling her son in her arms. He was wrapped in a blue blanket and had tear-stained chubby cheeks. "What?"

Mr. Hall held the phone up to her face. "It is her, isn't it?"

Mrs. Hall seemed puzzled for a moment before she responded. "Michele, yes, that's her. Why?"

Kayli's tense shoulders sagged in relief. *At last! A bloody name!* "Michele what? How do you know her?"

"It's Michele Granger. She's our babysitter."

Kayli was in shock. "How long have you known her?"

Mr. Hall led his wife over to the couch and forced her to sit down beside him. "At least six months. Maybe more. Why?"

"We believe that she abducted a three-year-old child yesterday. Plus, we also think she might be connected to another case we're investigating."

"No. I don't believe it." Sharon shook her head in disbelief. "I can't believe she would be guilty of such a thing. She's a lovely girl."

"Can you give us her phone number and address? We need to have a chat with her if only to discount her from our enquiries."

"Of course. Mike, get me my phone. It's in my handbag in the kitchen."

Her husband flew out of the room and returned seconds later, carrying her handbag.

"I have my hands full. You'll have to search for it," she instructed her husband when he dangled the bag in front of her.

Kayli took the bag from him. "I'll get it." She withdrew the phone and placed the bag on the floor by Sharon's feet. "Here it is. Her number and her address."

Dave took down the details in his notebook.

"How did you get in contact with her in the first place?" Kayli asked.

"I spotted a notice in the local newsagent's. Are you telling me that she killed Sophie?"

"It's pure conjecture at this time. We'll know more once we've spoken to her. Please, do not contact her. No matter how tempted you might be. Leave us to deal with this, okay?"

Mr. Hall's eyes narrowed. "Okay, as much as I want to go round there and wring her bloody neck, I'll refrain from doing so. Don't let her get away with this, Inspector. My God, the parents of the three-year-old must be going out of their minds with worry. What a bitch! She always came across as a nice girl. Although I did catch her here once with her boyfriend in the house."

"You never told me that, Mike."

"Sorry, love. I nipped back one day—forgot my wallet—and they were at it on the couch. I was livid and kicked him out right away. Shit! Do you think that's why she did it? Revenge?"

Kayli shrugged. "We won't know if or why she did this until we find her. Can you describe the boyfriend?"

"He had longish blond hair, skinny. About my height: six-one. I can't tell you anything more than that, sorry."

"It's better than nothing. I'm sure it will help. Look, I want to thank you for taking the time to speak with us today. I'm truly sorry for your loss. We'll head off and begin our investigation in earnest now that we can put a name to her face, thanks to your help."

"I hope you pick the bitch up soon, Inspector."

"So do I, Mr. Hall," Kayli said, then she and Dave shook his hand at the front door and walked towards the car.

"What now? Do you think there could be a link? Both fathers being cabbies, I mean?" Dave asked through gritted teeth.

"Hmm... Possibly. We could look into that side of things. Right now, I think we should rein our emotions in and consider our next move carefully. The last thing I want to do is charge over there and scare her into doing something terrible with the other missing children, if she has them. My take is she's in cahoots with the boyfriend. We need to find out his name and delve into his background."

"What about asking her neighbours, see if they can give us any more details to go on? Perhaps they can tell us what vehicle he drives. It would be a start, right?"

Kayli drove to Michele's neighbourhood with mixed emotions, buoyed that they at last had a name to go on, yet also terrified that a teenage girl, not a woman as they first thought, could be as heartless and brutal as her. Kayli's concern for the missing children heightened during the journey.

## 15

After questioning the neighbours, Kayli and Dave combatted the heavy flow of traffic and arrived back at the station around three.

Kayli brought the team up to date swiftly. "Only one of the neighbours could remember the boyfriend and that he drove a white van. I think we're definitely on the right lines now. Michele hasn't been seen at her address for a day or two, according to the same neighbour. He didn't ring the station last night when he recognised her image because he was worried she would retaliate. He says she's a mouthy cow, and yet Sophie's parents said she was a lovely girl."

"So why the change of heart?" Donna asked.

"Maybe us showing up on his doorstep jabbed at his conscience. I told him we were dealing with two cases where young children had been murdered."

"Something else came to mind while you were out, boss."

"Go on, Donna."

"Have you contacted the Watsons recently? I can't remember if you've shown them Michele's image or not?"

"I haven't—you're spot on. I'll give Kelvin a call. If the family are out of hospital, I'll ask him to come in and see me. Actually, the neighbour's reaction still rankles me. I think we should set up a surveillance on Michele's flat. Any volunteers?"

Graeme raised his hand. "I don't mind. Lindy said she's going out with the girls this evening anyway."

Kayli's stomach twisted. Graeme's girlfriend, Lindy, was Kayli's best friend, yet she hadn't been invited to join her. *A sign that I've neglected my friends of late, what with all the hassle at home. I need to get back out there socialising again before I become staid and old.* "That reminds me... I need to give Lindy a call to catch up."

He nodded. "She mentioned the other day that you hadn't been in touch. I'll tell her you're thinking of her. What if Michele turns up at the house?"

"Don't approach her. We just need to keep her under observation for now. Neither of the neighbours mentioned seeing anyone else going in the house, only Michele and this boyfriend of hers. We need to find out where they're hiding the kids first before we pick her up."

"Want me to get over there now, boss?"

"If you don't mind. Can you pull an all-nighter and report back here first thing, Graeme?"

"Sure. No problem."

"Right, I have a call to make. Several, in fact." Kayli marched into her office and closed the door. She searched for Kelvin's number and punched it into her phone. He answered the call virtually straight away. "Kelvin, it's DI Bright, just ringing up to see how everyone is."

"Oh, hi. We're fine. All out of hospital now. Staying in a hotel until we can start cleaning up the house. The insurers are refusing to pay out because it was an arson attack. We can't stay in a hotel indefinitely; the cost is exorbitant."

"What about family members? Your brother's place, perhaps?"

"I'd rather not. I'll take care of my family in my own way, Inspector."

"Okay, I was wondering, as you're out of hospital, if you could drop by the station to see me. Today, if possible. I realise it's short notice."

"I could be there within the hour. I have some spare time before my shift starts this evening. I'm just twiddling my thumbs here anyway."

"Great. I'll see you then. Thanks, Kelvin." Kayli disconnected the call and immediately dialled Naomi's number.

"What can I do for you, Kayli?"

"Is it too early for you to give me an assessment on the PM you carried out on the child discovered today. I have a name for you, by the way. Sophie Hall."

"Glad you've managed to identify her. Have the parents been informed?"

Kayli sighed. "Yes. I've told them you'll be in touch once you've completed your examination."

"Thanks. As with the Watson girl, there was no significant DNA found at the scene."

"That's a shame, although I'm pretty confident we can link the crimes, as we've identified at least one of the suspects, possibly two of them, in common between the two cases. Not sure how much they're involved at this stage or if they're the main players."

"You're not making much sense. Want to run that past me again?" Naomi said.

"Okay, a witness at Jamillia's school worked with a sketch artist and came up with the image of a young woman. Yesterday, a three-year-old girl was snatched from a play area close to Jamillia's school. When Dave knocked on a few doors in the area to see if anyone had seen the incident, he showed the picture of the young woman, and the witness positively identified her. In both incidences, a white van was used to transport the victims. Last night, I managed to persuade the media to run the image of both the abducted little girl and the image of the young woman. Today, I found out that the woman's name is Michele Granger. She was Sophie's babysitter."

"Wow, you *have* been busy. Babysitter? How deplorable! You think you can trust people with your kids, and they turn around and do this."

"I know. It doesn't bear thinking about. If I had kids, I don't think I'd ever trust anyone else with their care."

"So, you'd have them around your neck twenty-four-seven? I think you'd soon change your mind about that, Kayli, after a day or two."

Kayli sniggered. "Okay, maybe you're right. Anyway, it's pure speculation right now, but we also believe Michele has a boyfriend who owns a white van. We have nothing more regarding that at this point. It's more than we had yesterday. I have Kelvin Watson coming in to see me this afternoon, and I'm hoping there's a connection there also. We just need to find this Michele. Hopefully, she'll lead us to where they're holding the missing children—if the others are still alive, that is."

"You need me to try and place either of the suspects at the scene in that case, I take it?"

"Exactly. How, I'm not sure. You said there was no DNA at either scene, right?"

"There might not have been DNA, but I found a partial footprint in the warehouse. It's a start. If we can identify the boyfriend, we can match the footprint, which will place him at the crime scene."

"Any idea when Jamillia's funeral is going to be?"

"No. The parents came to see her. I've asked if we can hold on to her for a week or so just in case anything else crops up. They were happy… maybe that was a bad choice of words. They agreed, said it would give them time to make all the arrangements. Weren't they involved in an arson attack?"

"Yep. They haven't had the easiest of times lately."

"Right, if there's nothing else, I'll finish typing up the PM report and send it through to you by the end of the day. I can revisit both girls' bodies tomorrow. At the moment, I have no PMs lined up. Of course, that could change overnight."

"That's brilliant. Thanks, Naomi. Speak to you soon if I stumble across anything else."

"Ditto, Kayli. Bye for now."

Kayli spent the next hour going over every minor detail they had to do with the case before the desk sergeant rang to inform her that Kelvin Watson was waiting in the reception area. She flew down the stairs like a woman possessed, slowing down to compose herself when she was close to the bottom. She breezed into the reception area and shook Kelvin's hand. "So nice to see you again. Glad your wife and daughter are both fit and well after your horrendous ordeal. Let's find a quiet room."

"Happy to help out where I can. You know that, Inspector."

Kayli called across the room. "Sergeant, is Interview Room One free?"

"It is, ma'am. Do you need any assistance?" The sergeant meant if she required a member of his staff to sit in on the interview.

"Not this time, thanks all the same."

She led the way down the narrow corridor, opened the door, and motioned for Kelvin to step inside the room ahead of her. He pulled out a chair and watched as she closed the door then joined him at the table, his eyes never leaving hers.

"Have I done something wrong, Inspector?"

"Not that I'm aware of, Kelvin. Have you?"

Holding her gaze, he shook his head. "It's just that you've always come to the house to see me. Granted, that's a little difficult at this moment in time, but you get my drift."

"Honestly, there is nothing for you to worry about. I just thought under the circumstances this would be a better meeting place than your hotel room."

He snorted. "You're not wrong there. Living on top of each other in a fifteen-foot-square room leaves a lot to be desired. It's like a tornado struck, and we're still picking up the pieces." His smile faded. "I suppose it has in one way. We miss Jamillia so much. I think it'll be even worse when we finally get back home after the clean-up has finished."

"How are you going to manage the clean-up with no assistance from your insurers?"

"We'll get there. The staff at work have been brilliant. They've agreed to chip in with their time in between shifts, plus Lorella's workmates have said they'll lend a hand when they can too. We're truly blessed to be surrounded by loving and caring people. Not sure how we would have coped otherwise. Sorry, I've prattled on enough. Can we get to the point of this visit?"

Kayli withdrew a copy of Michele's image and placed it on the table in front of him.

His head jutted forward, and with wide eyes, he glanced up at her. "What about her?"

"Do you know her? I'm guessing by your reaction that you do."

"Yes, I know her. Michele Granger. What about her, Inspector?" He thrust the paper away from him.

"Well, one of your neighbours gave me the impression that she thinks there is something going on between the two of you—is there?" His elbows landed on the table with a thud and he covered his face with his hands. "Kelvin, it would be better if you didn't lie to me. Is it fact or fiction?"

"It was a one-off. I don't know why I did it."

Kayli felt let down by this man—a man she was desperately trying to help. "When did it happen? Where?"

"At the house, a few months ago. It was when Lorella was on a night out with the girls. I nipped back to the house during one of my shifts. I'd forgotten some paperwork for my boss. I entered the house, popped my head in the lounge to tell Michele why I was there, and ran upstairs. When I came down again, I opened the lounge door to find her standing naked in the middle of the room, dancing. I asked her what she was playing at, and she sauntered over to me and began undressing me."

"And you didn't stop her?"

"I was mesmerised by the tautness of her body and the thought of having sex with her."

"Wow, is that all it took for you to be unfaithful to Lorella? Is your wife aware of your affair?"

He slammed a clenched fist onto the table. "It was *not* an affair, and no, Lorella isn't aware of the incident. I'd rather you not tell her, either. It was a mistake. The worst mistake I've ever made. It hurts my heart and my head whenever I relive the events of that day. It was ten minutes—that's all, Inspector. You have to believe me."

"Ten minutes or ten hours, it amounts to the same thing, Kelvin. You cheated on your wife."

"I know, and I have regretted it every day since."

"I have the feeling that regret is about to multiply tenfold when you hear what I have to tell you."

"I don't understand. What's going on?"

"I take it you didn't see the local news bulletin last night?"

"No. I worked last night. You're aware of my shift hours. Why? What did I miss?"

"A plea for anyone who knows this young woman to come forward, along with a picture of a three-year-old girl we believe she abducted yesterday."

He flung himself back in his chair and linked the fingers of both hands on top of his head. "Are you serious?"

Kayli leaned forward in her chair and narrowed her eyes. "I've never been more bloody serious in my life, Mr. Watson. Now, tell me what you know about the woman you had ten-minute sex with behind your wife's back."

His hands slipped down and covered his face, trying to hide his sobs. Her heart went out to him for a second or two until she reprimanded herself. *If it wasn't for this man's selfish actions his daughter probably would be alive today.* Fortunately, she wasn't cold-hearted enough to voice her opinion out loud, given the emotional turmoil he was putting himself through.

"What have I done?" he repeated several times.

"We need to get past this quickly, Kelvin. This girl is on the loose and has another innocent child within her grasp. Tell me what you know about Michele."

He inhaled a large breath to compose himself and wiped his eyes on his jacket sleeve. "Not much I can tell you, really."

"*Try*! There must be something. How did she become your babysitter?"

"I spotted a card in the newsagent's window. Lorella had recently said that she wanted more freedom, and with me working the night shift... well, I couldn't look after the kids myself. Lorella was a bit of a party-goer before we hooked up. She was missing the clubbing scene, and even though she loved the kids, she said she wanted to get out more. I arranged for Michele to come round to see us. It was a joint decision to take her on, but I still feel responsible for suggesting her in the first place. We thought she was an ideal candidate for the job, as she was enrolled in a childcare course at the local uni. At least that's what she told us during the interview."

Kayli scribbled down the information in her notebook. "Anything else? Did she talk about her boyfriend at all?"

"I wasn't aware that she had one at the time. My God, do you think she abducted Jamillia out of some kind of revenge? She wanted us to do it again, but I refused."

"We're not sure. The teaching assistant at the school worked with the sketch artist and came up with that." Kayli pointed at the drawing lying between them. "We believe she's not only responsible for abducting and killing Jamillia, but also another girl whose body was found in a warehouse yesterday."

"Are you saying she's some kind of serial killer?"

"Maybe. My take is that she might be part of a paedophile ring, but I've yet to discover the evidence to prove that. At this stage, we're assuming that the boyfriend is involved as it would appear his van has been used in a couple of the cases as a getaway vehicle."

He shook his head. "Why? Why choose innocent kids?"

"It's what these types of predators do, Kelvin. They use people who are unsuspecting to infiltrate the families—then bang! As Michele is so young, I believe there is probably another person higher up dictating her every move. Either that or she's more twisted than we're giving her credit for. Either way, we need to stop her from taking more children. Three more children have been reported missing in the area and we think she might have them. Did she ever mention another address that she uses?"

"No. She's never discussed details of her address with me. I only ever had her phone number. This is unbelievable. What the hell am I going to tell Lorella? First, she'll be mortified, and then she'll want to go round there and beat the crap out of her. Jesus, what a mess! To think that animal wormed her way into our affections only to have one intention in mind. That poor child… a three-year-old, you say? I don't even want to bloody imagine what these people will consider doing to her." He retched but managed to hold back from being sick.

"Are you all right, Kelvin?"

"Sick to my stomach. Not sure I'll ever be all right again, if you must know. Why pick on me and my family?"

"You answered the advert. Can you tell me the name of the newsagent?"

"No point. I was in there the other day and read the cards in the window. Hers wasn't there."

"At least that's one thing. It also raises another question, of why she's stopped advertising. I'd still like the address of the newsagent." She offered him her notebook, and he jotted down the address then slid it back to her.

"Can I go now?"

Kayli smiled. "Yes, go home. Make sure you give your wife and Marcia a hug when you get home. We should never forget how precious life is. I know it's going to be difficult, but you need to put this behind you and focus on Lorella and Marcia from this day forward. I'm not saying forget about Jamillia, just that there is no point feeling guilty about the situation. It won't accomplish anything in the long run."

"Thank you. Not sure I agree with the guilt bit. I think that is going to live with me for a long time."

After Kayli saw him off, she walked slowly up the stairs to the incident room, contemplating what their next move should be.

Donna turned to look at her when she entered the door. "Boss, I think I have something."

Kayli rushed towards her, hopefulness surging through her like a tidal wave. "What's that, Donna?"

"I was going through the calls that came in after the TV appeal, and this one caught my eye." She thrust a slip of paper at Kayli.

Reading the note, she frowned thoughtfully. "Someone thinks they saw her at a concert? Does that seem right to you?"

"Not sure… maybe."

"Okay, nothing this girl has done really makes sense to date, so maybe we shouldn't discount it. You know what I'm going to say next, right?"

"You want me to track down the CCTV footage, see if I can spot the van."

"You've got it. If we can get a licence plate, we can put uniform on alert at least."

"On it now."

"Anything else of interest in amongst that lot, Donna?"

"Nothing noteworthy. I'll get back to you soon, I hope."

Kayli turned to address the rest of the team. "I have a few calls to make. Kelvin told me that he believes Michele Granger was enrolled in a childcare course at uni. She might not be at home now, but she could still be attending class. It's worth a shot. I'd rather look in to it than regret it later on. When I asked him about how he made contact with Michele in the first place, he said it was through an advert for babysitting duties that she placed in a newsagent's window."

"Is it still there? Didn't Sophie's dad say the same thing?" Dave asked.

"He did. Kelvin said he looked at the ads in the newsagent's a few days ago, but couldn't see the card. Here's the address. Give them a ring, Dave. Can you also ring all the newsagents in the area, see if they're running the advert or remember displaying the advert a few weeks ago?"

"And what if they do?"

"I don't know. See if they know the girl, if she lives close by, that type of thing. Don't forget we're looking for another address where they could be holding the children. If we don't ask the questions we're unlikely to locate that address, right?"

"Gotcha. Sorry for being so dense."

"You're not being dense. This is a tough one to call, and sometimes we're going to have to think outside the box. One more snippet of information you need to know is that Kelvin said he had a fling with Michele."

"What? You've got to be joking? I thought he was a nailed-on family man. Just goes to prove you can't judge a book."

"Yeah, it came as a shock to me. He's guilt-ridden. Not only because he was the one who spotted the advert, but also because he cheated on his wife."

"You reckon that's what this is about? Revenge?"

"I think so, don't you? Sophie's parents said pretty much the same thing. The father went berserk because she'd brought the boyfriend into their home. Maybe she hates being in the wrong in certain people's eyes, or hates any form of criticism or moral shaming. That would be my guess. What we need to do is try and locate her parents. She's in her late teens, granted she might not be from the area. Just because she's attending university here, it doesn't mean that her family live in the area."

"Want me to look into that?" Dave asked.

"No. I want you to concentrate on the newsagents. I think going to visit the university will give us the contact details for her parents. Also, we have her phone number. As much as I'm tempted to ring it, I think we should see if we can get a trace on the phone."

"Good thinking. I can have a word with my mate in the tech department, see what he can come up with if you like?"

"Great, do that, Dave." Kayli walked towards the office and called over her shoulder, "Good luck, guys. I sense we're closing in on them. I hope they're not thinking along the same lines."

## 16

Blackbird drove to the cottage during his lunchbreak. He'd been anxious at work all morning. He hated dealing with inept people, and the youngsters were proving they were at the top of the list in that department. After parking the car next to the van, he snuck around the back of the building, straining to listen to what was going on inside. It was unusually quiet. That made him wary. Were they about to ambush him? *Don't be so foolish... why would they do that? They'd be lost without me pulling their strings.*

He turned the handle on the back door, but the door didn't open like it usually did. He rapped his knuckles on the flaking paint.

Swift's face appeared at the kitchen window above the sink before he opened the door.

"What's going on?" Blackbird demanded.

Swift prodded him in the chest before he even had a chance to close the door. "This is your fault."

"What is?"

"She refuses to go out now after that image appeared on the TV last night."

Confused, Blackbird shook his head. "How is that my fault?"

"If you'd kept your mouth shut about it, she'd be none the wiser, but no, you had to stick your nose in and blab about it. Now she's too petrified to even venture out."

"Don't be ridiculous. Firstly, it's not my fault her face is all over the news. It's *her* fault for letting that witness see her, and secondly, you two need to frigging up your game. Haven't you ever heard of wearing a bloody disguise?" He flung his arms up in the air. "Why the hell do I have to do your thinking for you as well as everything else around here? Where is she?"

"Downstairs, feeding the girls."

"Hallelujah! At least that's a first."

"Cut the sarcasm. We're doing our best around here. It's hard being forced to live here day and night. This place is a shithole."

"It wasn't until you arrived. Try cleaning the place up now and again."

"I didn't realise you had OCD, as well," Swift replied sarcastically.

"I haven't, but even I know how much rats and other creepy crawlies are attracted to smells such as this. It stinks in here."

The door to the cellar opened, and Magpie glared at him before she closed the door. "Nice of you to finally turn up."

"What? You weren't expecting me until this evening. Not sure why I bothered wasting my lunch hour to come here when all I get in return is verbal abuse."

"You coming here once a day is enough for me, man," Magpie shouted.

He raised his hands in front of him. "Whoa! Either you back off, bitch, or I walk away for good and take my list of contacts with me."

Magpie flung herself into the chair, and a look of defeat draped itself around her shoulders. "I'm sorry. Ignore me. I hate being holed up here. I might as well be in a cage like them downstairs."

"Now you're being stupid," Swift chastised her.

*It could be arranged, bitch. You keep getting on my nerves the way you are.* "Stop feeling sorry for yourself. It ain't gonna wash with me." Blackbird sat at the table, and clearing his throat, motioned for Swift to join them. "I've had a long think about the situation, and here's my conclusion. I didn't sign up to snatching three-year-olds, so here's what's going to happen."

Swift opened his mouth to speak, but Blackbird raised a hand to silence him.

"Let me finish. I'm here for the next three quarters of an hour. In that time, we need to come up with a strategy to get that child back to her mother. If you start quibbling about it, I'm going to walk away from here and never come back."

Swift laughed so hard, his head tipped back. "You really ain't thought that pathetic statement through, have you? You're forgetting you own this fuckin' gaff."

Blackbird glared at him, and a twitch began at the corner of his eye. *Shit! He's right!* "What I meant to say is that I'll show you the door, and we'll part ways. You've overstepped the mark, and I want out. You're becoming unpredictable. I never know what I'm going to come back here and find next."

"That's tough shit, man! At the end of the day, we're our own people. If we want to change the route we take, then that's up to us," Swift replied angrily.

"Then that's why we need to go our separate ways. It's obvious that we want different things from this situation. I'm under strict instructions not to obtain girls younger than seven." The pair sitting opposite him fell silent. He had them by the short and curlies. It was time to issue his ultimate blow. "Therefore, I'm giving you until seven this evening to get rid of the kid. Preferably by returning her to her mother, not by killing her."

"Aw, man. You realise how difficult that is going to be?"

"You should have thought about that when you veered away from the plan. It's up to you two to rectify the situation before we can move on and finalise the delivery of the other girls."

Magpie placed her head in her hands and screamed. "Stop it! I know we screwed up. We'll deal with it this afternoon. We'll take the girl back and leave her in the park where we stole her from."

Swift dug her in the ribs. "We can't do that. The police will be watching the area like hawks. I've got no intention of being caught this late in the game."

Blackbird rose from his chair. "Then there's nothing more to say. I have to get back to work. Either that girl is gone by the time I get back, or I'm ending this relationship, and no money will be coming your way, because you two broke the contract."

"You think you're so smart, don't ya? There was no friggin' contract, man."

"The agreement we put in place then. So, what's it to be?"

"We'll do it this afternoon. The trouble is we don't have the girl's address."

Blackbird's arms spread out to the side. "You could always ask her. It's one of the first things parents generally instil into their children at a very young age."

Magpie tore open the door to the cellar and ran down the stairs. Blackbird and Swift listened to her trying to coax the address out of the child before she began shouting at her. Furious, Blackbird rushed down the stairs after her and yanked her away from the cage. "Leave her to me. Get out of here." Magpie stomped her way back upstairs again, leaving him to deal with the sea of frightened faces.

Tears glistened on Belinda's cheeks. He beckoned her with his finger. "Come here, Belinda." Two of the girls tried to hold her back, protecting her, but Blackbird sneered at them. "Let her go."

They instantly dropped their hands. He beckoned Belinda again with his finger. Her head turned to either side as if to check with the other girls to see if it was okay to continue. They both nodded. Belinda shuffled forward on the floor.

Blackbird whispered, "Belinda, if you tell me where you live, I promise you'll go home today."

The others gasped. One of them asked, "What about us? Can we go home too?"

Blackbird smiled. "Eventually, girls. Come on, Belinda, tell me."

Belinda mumbled her address then scooted back to sit with the other girls. Feeling smug, as another piece of his plan slotted into place, Blackbird left the room and closed the door behind him. After giving the youngsters Belinda's address, he asked, "When? When will you be dropping her off?"

Swift glared at him. "When we choose."

"Right, I'll leave it with you then. I'll be back later, as promised. She better not still be there, or there'll be trouble."

Magpie sighed heavily. "But I don't want to leave here. What if I'm seen?"

"Get a disguise. You have to deliver the girl this afternoon. Got that?" He refused to listen to any more of their excuses and left the house. He heard the key move in the lock behind him. Once he was out of sight of the cottage, he placed the call to the police from a phone box by the side of the road. *Two kids killed already, it's the unpredictability I can't stand. You guys have really overstepped the mark this time and are now going to pay for your stupidity.*

"DI Bright, now!"

"Who's calling?"

"Just put her on the line," he snapped, covering the mouthpiece of the phone with a hanky to muffle his voice.

"DI Kayli Bright. How can I help?"

"The girl will be delivered to her parents today."

"What girl? Who are you?"

"Less of the questions. You know what girl I'm referring to. Don't piss me off."

"Delivered to her address by whom?"

"The idiots who took her. That's all you need to know." He hung up, ran back to his car, and put his foot on the accelerator in case the police managed to trace the call.

~

"Crap!" Kayli ran out of her office, breathless with excitement. "I've just had a tip-off to say the girl—I'm assuming they meant Belinda—is going to be delivered back to her mother today."

"That's excellent news. Are you going to lay a trap, boss?" Dave asked.

"Wouldn't that be dicey?" Donna replied.

Kayli nodded. "I agree with Donna. Ideally, we want the kidnappers to lead us back to where they're keeping the other girls. Graeme is already out there. I'll make him aware of the situation, tell him to shoot over to Rachel's house, it's not far, plus get some unmarked cars in the area to help him follow the kidnappers once the drop has been made. I really don't want to alert the mother about this in case it was someone playing a warped practical joke on us."

"I wonder how the person who contacted you knows what's going on. Unless they're involved," Donna said, asking and answering her own question.

"That's my take on it, Donna. Maybe displaying Michele's picture on TV had the desired effect and a member of the team is on the turn. We won't know until we capture Michele and, hopefully, her boyfriend," Kayli said, heading for the vending machine to buy everyone a coffee.

Dave tapped the side of his face with a pencil. "Maybe it's the boyfriend who made the call. Pissed off with her and wanting out. Maybe he found out that Kelvin slept with her."

"You could be right, Dave. Any luck with tracing the girl's phone or with the newsagents?"

"I've called all the newsagents in the area. Some of them remembered a girl placing an advert in their shop windows, but they withdrew the ad when she didn't renew it. None of them recognised her."

"Which leads me to think she's not local and why I need to visit the university. Dave, I think you should stay here. I'll shoot over there by myself."

"If that's what you want, boss."

"I'll drink this and call Graeme then make a move. I have a good feeling about this, guys. Let's keep the momentum going. I have a feeling the case will be coming to an end soon." She rushed back into the office and picked up the phone. "Graeme, it's me. There's been a development." Kayli made him aware of the call she'd received and told him to go to Rachel's house to keep a vigilant eye open for the next few hours. Graeme seemed as buoyant about the information as she was. He promised to call her as soon as anything happened at his end.

Looking at the overcast weather through the window, she hitched on her coat then hurried from the station with Donna and Dave's best wishes ringing in her ears as she descended the stairs and jumped in the car. Twenty minutes later, she pulled up outside the university and parked in the first available space she could find in the nearby road.

The receptionist greeted her with a warm smile. Producing her warrant card, Kayli asked to see the person in charge.

A man standing at the filing cabinet a few feet away from the receptionist glanced at Kayli. "I'm the Dean. Will I do?"

Kayli nodded. "You will, indeed. Is there somewhere private where we can go to have a brief chat regarding one of your pupils? I'd ask my questions here, but there's no telling who might overhear our conversation."

"Of course." He opened a panel in the counter to let her through. "My office is just back here." The room was what she'd expected in such surroundings. Bookshelves lined one of the walls, and a desk made from a dark wood she didn't recognise was positioned in front of the window. "Please take a seat. Sorry, I didn't catch your name. My name is Terry O'Donnell."

"I'm DI Kayli Bright of the Avon and Somerset Constabulary."

"Pleased to meet you, Inspector. Now, what was it you wanted to speak to me about, or should I say who?"

"A Michele Granger. I've been reliably informed that she's enrolled in a childcare course here at the university."

"Obviously, I'll have to check. Just a moment." He picked up the phone and asked the receptionist to bring in the girl's attendance file.

The door opened after a light tap. "The file you requested, sir. Can I get you both a drink?"

Kayli shook her head. "That's very kind. Not for me, thank you."

"I'll leave it, as well. Thank you, Jill."

The receptionist left, and Terry flipped open the file. "Ah yes, what is it you'd like to know about this young lady?"

"First of all, I need to know what her attendance has been like recently." Kayli withdrew her notebook and pen.

"By the looks of things, very patchy." He seemed annoyed by the revelation. "May I ask what your interest is in this student?"

Kayli chewed on the inside of her mouth for a second. "We're investigating several serious crimes in the area and believe she is linked to those crimes. In what capacity, we're not totally sure as yet."

"Really? Can you tell me what type of crimes, Inspector?"

She cringed, hoping that he wouldn't press her further to reveal the truth. "I'd rather not say at this point. I'd hate to tarnish her name with you if it turns out the information I've been given is wrong."

He fidgeted in his chair. "Do you need anything else?"

"Her parents' or next of kin's address, if you would. That'd be a great help."

Terry flicked through several pages and tapped one page in particular with his finger. "She's actually from Newcastle."

"Wow, is it common for students to live that far away from home?"

He laughed. "Some would say the farther, the better. Here it is, if you need to copy down the address."

Kayli took the paper and wrote out the address. "All right if I take the phone number too?"

"Of course. Do you think the parents will be able to help you?"

"I'm hoping so. Only time will tell. Do you know if Michele has a boyfriend?"

"I'm not sure. I could contact her lecturer and ask the question."

"That would be very helpful. Maybe you'll allow me to speak to a couple of her fellow students, if that's possible?"

"Shall we see what information you gather from her lecturer first, then go from there? I'd rather not get anyone else involved at this time."

"Sure, I'm agreeable to that." She watched the Dean pick up the phone and place another call.

"Miss Jackson will be here shortly, Inspector."

The room filled with an eerie silence until there was a knock on the door.

"Come in," Terry shouted.

A petite woman wearing a tartan suit entered the room. Her gaze shot between Kayli and the Dean. "Hello, sir. You wanted to see me?"

"Come in, Miss Jackson. This is DI Bright of Avon and Somerset Constabulary. She'd like to ask you some questions about one of your students, a Michele Granger," he said, looking down at the file to check the girl's name.

"Hmm... Miss Granger seems to be a law unto herself. I'm sure another student would have been delighted to have filled her shoes on the course."

"I've looked over her attendance record. Maybe her lack of attendance should have been brought to my attention sooner."

"I'm sorry. That's my fault entirely, sir. I don't take pleasure in getting the students into trouble if I can avoid it."

"That's all well and good, but according to the inspector here, this young lady has been up to no good in the eyes of the law. That's not something the university likes to be associated with, Miss Jackson."

"I'm sorry, sir. I take full responsibility."

Kayli cleared her throat. "I'm sorry to interrupt. However, it's imperative that I get back to the station as soon as possible."

"What has Granger done? May I ask?" Miss Jackson asked, her brow deeply furrowed.

"We believe she's involved in some very serious crimes...against children."

Miss Jackson and Terry stared at each other.

"What sort of crimes?" Miss Jackson eventually asked.

"I can't go into detail, and to be honest, you really wouldn't want to hear the gruesome details anyway. What I need to know is if you're aware if she has a boyfriend and if so, what his name is."

"Oh my. Gosh, I wish I could help, but I tend not to get that involved in the students' personal lives."

"That's frustrating to hear, but understandable. Does she have a close friend in her class? Someone I can see to ask a few discreet questions perhaps?"

"Cindy Munroe I suppose would fall into that category," Miss Jackson offered.

"Would it be possible for me to have a quick word with her? Nothing too invasive, I promise. We just need to know who the boyfriend is and where he lives. I wouldn't be asking if I didn't feel it was important."

"I'm agreeable to that," the Dean said, letting out a large sigh. "Appalling that a student taking a childcare course should then go out and deliberately harm kids. Has she ever caused you to doubt her during a lecture, Miss Jackson?"

"Not that I can think of. I would say that her focus appeared to waver now and again, far more than the other girls in the class."

"Interesting. Maybe she attended the lessons as some form of cover-up to her actions. We've yet to get to the bottom of a lot of things regarding why Michele has done what she's done."

"Okay, let's get this organised then. I believe there's a spare room available along the hallway here. Miss Jackson, would you mind collecting the friend and asking her to join us please?"

Kayli raised a pointed finger. "Can you not mention what the meeting is about? I prefer to catch people unaware when I question them."

"Of course. I'll see you in a moment." Miss Jackson swiftly left the room.

Kayli sat opposite a stunned-looking Dean. "Are you all right?"

"Not really, Inspector. I can't say I've ever had anything like this brought to my attention before, and I've been here over twenty years. Are you saying that this girl has killed children?"

Kayli grimaced. "I'm sorry. I really can't answer that question."

He shook his head, and his eyes narrowed in anger. "I'm taking that as a yes then. Bloody hell! Never in my wildest dreams would I ever think one of my students could be guilty of such a crime."

"I have to correct you there. We believe at this point only that she is involved in the crimes. Loosely or otherwise remains to be seen."

"Even so, it's still disgusting in my book. An utter abomination."

"I agree. I have no idea how I'm going to break the news to her parents when the time comes. Can you direct me to the room?"

"Of course, I'll show you where it is personally. Good luck with questioning her friend, finding Granger, and informing what she's been doing to her parents. I don't envy you that task in the slightest."

"Thanks, it's definitely something I'll have to prepare myself for. I want to thank you for your assistance."

They left the office and walked down the corridor side by side. "Let's hope it doesn't prove to be a wasted trip for you."

Kayli smiled and raised her crossed fingers.

He opened the door and switched on the light. "Make yourself comfy. They shouldn't be too long." He left her alone in the room.

Kayli paced the floor until the door opened again a few minutes later when Miss Jackson and a girl in her late teens walked in.

"This is Cindy Munroe, Inspector. She's one of Michele's best friends here at uni."

"Thank you both for coming to see me. Shall we take a seat?"

"What do you need to see me for? And just to put things straight, I'm just a friend of Michele's. I'm not her best friend."

"Thank you for clearing that up, Cindy. Please, don't be nervous. I want to ask you a few questions. If that's okay?"

"I'm here, aren't I?" the young woman said sourly.

"For that, I'm very grateful," Kayli said, smiling to break down the barrier that had developed between them already. "Can you tell me the name of Michele's boyfriend?"

Cindy leaned back in her chair and folded her arms. "Not until you tell me what Michele is supposed to have done wrong."

"I'm sorry, but I can't discuss that."

Cindy unfolded her arms, huffed and stood up.

"Sit down, Cindy!" Miss Jackson said, her tone more threatening than angry, and the girl slumped into her chair again. "Now answer the inspector truthfully. Don't forget there is an exam coming up next week."

"You wouldn't dare! That's blackmail, Miss. Shame on you—in front of a copper too."

*The Missing Children*

"You really do have a smart mouth, don't you?" Kayli interjected with a glare.

"Not usually, but when it comes to my friends, I refuse to tell tales."

"I'm not asking you to. All I need is a name, and then you can go."

"Karl Freeman."

"There, that was simple enough. Do you happen to know where he lives?"

"You said all you wanted was a name. I've supplied that. Now I'd like to go."

Kayli shrugged. "Okay, I can't force you to tell me. I appreciate you giving me his name, though. I'd like to ask you not to contact Michele regarding this conversation."

"I don't keep anything from my friend, so that ain't going to happen."

"Okay, then I'll have no alternative but to tell Michele, when we catch up with her, who supplied me with her boyfriend's name." *Touché! Stick that where the sun don't shine, girly!*

"You can't do that."

"As far as I know, there is no law against what I'm prepared to do, although if you tell Michele that you've spoken to me, then there is such a charge as being an accessory to a crime." Her peripheral vision showed Miss Jackson covering a smile with her hand.

Cindy's mouth gaped open. "Jesus, it's true what they say about coppers twisting your words."

"Not at all. Your friend and her boyfriend have carried out some serious crimes. They are very dangerous criminals. If you want to be associated with them, then that's entirely your call, but I'm warning you, these kinds of relationships rarely end happily."

"I don't know what you're on about. Michele wouldn't do anything against the law."

"How can you be so sure about that? How long have you known her?"

"Just over a year. This is our second year on the course together."

"I suggest you choose your friends more carefully in future. I refuse to go into detail, but if I were you, I would make sure I didn't have anything to do with her again. I'm sure Miss Jackson would agree with that sentiment."

"Too right. Hopefully, the menace will be off the streets soon enough so the decision if Cindy wants to continue being Michele's friend or not will be taken out of her hands."

"Let's hope so. Thank you for your help, ladies. I need to get back on the hunt for Michele now. Cindy, bear in mind that I never make idle threats. If word gets back to Michele about this meeting, I know where to find you. Goodbye." Kayli rushed out of the room, and immediately rang Graeme from the car park. "Any news, mate?"

"Nothing as yet, boss. You'll be the first to know."

"Speak soon, I hope." She hung up and drove back to base, her mind whirling with how the case had progressed during the day.

She marched up the stairs and through the incident room door without acknowledging any of her colleagues who'd said hello during her journey. "Donna, I need you to look up a Karl Freeman for me. I want the usual—his address and if he has a record to his name."

"Who's that, boss?" Dave shouted from his desk.

"Michele Granger's boyfriend. It might be where they're hiding the kids. I called Graeme on the way over here. They've not shown up there yet. I sure hope this isn't a ploy to keep us busy so they can grab another child during the distraction."

"What can we do to ensure that doesn't happen?"

Kayli shook her head. "Nothing. Let's try and remain positive about this. Negativity serves no purpose. I'll be in my office. Give me a shout when you've located the dirt on Karl, Donna."

"Will do, boss."

That shout came sooner than Kayli expected. She ran out of her office and joined Dave, who was already sitting next to Donna, shaking his head at what he was reading on the monitor.

"What have you found?"

"His address is a small bedsit, boss. I doubt he'd have the room to keep the kids there. I also have a rap sheet for him. He's a petty criminal, nothing major. He was pulled over by a patrol car in a stop-and-

*The Missing Children*

search where a knife was found under the driver's seat. He denied it was his, but the vehicle was registered in his name. He was given a verbal warning."

"That means we've got a registration number for his vehicle, yes?"

Donna pointed to the screen. "Yep. Do you want me to start circulating it?"

"Too right. But I need you to add a caution not to approach the vehicle. We need to be mindful that they have these children hidden somewhere. It could be in a cave for all we know. The last thing we need is to arrest the buggers only for them to remain silent about where the kids are. That's happened before, right? I refuse to have that kind of shit flung at us. Let's do all we can to locate the children and uncover who else is involved. Any news about Michele's phone yet, Dave?"

"Nothing, very disappointing. Maybe she's changed it recently or used a different one to put her number around the newsagents."

"Maybe, keep trying. What about where the call came in from? Has anyone been out to the phone box to see its location?"

Dave grimaced. "I'll get on it straight away. Sorry, I should have thought about that myself."

"I don't want apologies, Dave. We need to ensure that any clues are dealt with appropriately. Especially when there are lives at risk."

"I hear you, sorry."

Kayli tutted. "Maybe we should put a surveillance on his bedsit anyway. With only a small team, that's kind of hard to do."

"I don't mind doing it. I'm only twiddling my fingers around here."

"Trouble is if we get a call from Graeme, I'll need you to come with me." Her mobile rang, and Graeme's name filled her screen. "Talk of the devil." She smiled and answered the call. "Hi, Graeme, what have you got?"

"The drop-off just occurred, boss. I'm in contact with an unmarked police vehicle who has taken up the chase. Thought I'd better take the girl in to her mother before setting off."

Kayli thumped the air. "Great news! You did the right thing. Are you able to join the chase now?"

"Already actioned, boss. I can see both vehicles up ahead."

M A COMLEY

"Keep your distance. Only apprehend the suspects once you think they're approaching where the kids are being kept, got that?"

"Whoops! Here we go. They've sussed we're following them, and he's put his damn foot down. What do you want us to do?"

"You're going to have to stick with him then, Graeme. Dave and I are on our way. I'm going to arrange for the eye in the sky to join us. Maybe they'll spot something we're unable to see from the ground."

"Rightio, boss. I'll keep you up-to-date on the radio in that case. Gotta fly."

"Any news on that phone box location, Dave?" Kayli asked.

"Yep, just got it. It's down a country lane, nice rural location."

"Brilliant. Get a patrol car out to the location immediately with a SOCO team. This could be the break we need, guys. Let's hit them hard and fast." Kayli clenched her fist in front of her, jubilant about what was going down. Then she placed the call to request the police chopper to get airborne.

Moments later, she and Dave ran down the stairs faster than an Olympian sprinter and out to the car. Kayli threw Dave the keys to her car. "You drive. That way I can keep track on what's going on better."

"If you trust me to drive your car, that's fine by me."

"Just avoid any scrapes wherever possible."

"Oh ye of little faith. I can't believe we're finally closing in on them."

"Believe it, Dave, because it's finally happening."

"Charlie One this is Bravo Nine. The stinger has been used. The van has been stopped. Two people in the vehicle have been apprehended. A man and a woman."

"Why? Why stop them now, Graeme?"

"They turned down a country lane, boss."

"Okay, we're on our way. Give me your exact location. Has the chopper been in touch?"

"He's here, circling overhead, boss."

"Put your foot down, Dave. We have a bunch of kids to find."

## 17

When Kayli and Dave arrived at the scene, they found a skinny young man with long blond hair tussling with two uniformed police officers, while a girl was sitting in the back of one of the patrol cars, her head dipped, feeling desperately sorry for herself. Graeme was in the front seat of the car, speaking to the girl.

"Karl Freeman, I take it?"

His eyes creased up at the sides, and it looked as though he was about to spit at her. "Who wants to know?"

Turning to the constables restraining him, Kayli asked, "Has he said where they're being held?"

"No, ma'am. He's not given us anything yet."

Dave stepped forward and grabbed the front of Freeman's T-shirt. "Maybe you and I should have a little chat in the back of your van."

"Yeah, and maybe you should go fuck yourself, man. Lay one finger on me, and I'll have you for assault."

Kayli purposefully remained quiet, pleased that Dave had taken over the reins but also wary in case her partner fulfilled his threat.

"You've obviously never heard of the term 'resisting arrest' then. You know what? It's surprising the amount of injuries criminals have suffered under that term. I'd be happy to add your name to the list." He winked at Freeman and inched closer.

With Dave a few inches taller, the youth's bravado wilted, and he visibly shrank before their eyes. "I know nothing. All I was doing was out for a ride with my girlfriend. Your lot damaged my vehicle with that death-trap. I wasn't aware that it was against the law to drive around Bristol, minding your own business."

Dave leaned into his personal space. "Keep winding me up, buddy, and I'll take pleasure in ripping you apart."

Seeing that Dave's strong-arm tactic was only giving the youth extra cockiness, Kayli pulled Dave out of the way and leaned in herself. "We've got all the evidence we need to put you and your scheming girlfriend away for years. Think you can treat us like idiots? Think again, moron. The first thing we're going to do is send your van to the forensic lab." He gulped. "Hadn't thought about that, had you? Every little girl you've abducted will have left some form of DNA in the back of your vehicle. Even the two that you've brutally tortured and killed." Every word spoken and the closeness to the bastard made Kayli angrier with each passing second.

"Bullshit, lady, and you know it."

Dave tried to muscle Kayli aside to deal with the disrespectful youth, but she stood her ground as the two constables on either side restrained him harder. She was desperate to have a slice of the little shit and his girlfriend. She had a feeling that the girl was going to talk freely back at the station once they were alone. She wasn't so sure about the cocky individual standing in front of her. As if her right hand had a will all of its own, she jabbed him in the eyes with two fingers.

"Hey, what the fuck? You lay one more finger on me and my solicitor is going to kick your arse for you."

"Is that right? I take it you don't take any heed from warnings given to you by a serving police officer then? Look around you, buddy. Each of these guys are anxious to have a piece of you. Paedophiles are the scum of this earth, and my colleagues always turn the other cheek when one is turned over. It's like an unspoken rule that comes with the job."

"I ain't one of them, bitch, and you've got nothing in the way of evidence to prove that either."

Kayli smiled. "You keep believing that, sonny, and they'll bang you up in an asylum where you belong. Of course, the beating I foresee you having in a few minutes and the time you're going to serve behind bars could be decreased if you admit your role."

"Making false statements like that ain't gonna change my mind, lady."

Kayli shrugged and shook her head. "You had your chance. Guys, I'll give you five minutes with the little shit. Why these perverts insist on resisting arrest truly is beyond my comprehension. I'll be over there speaking to the other suspect. Let me know when you think he's ready to talk."

Dave laughed. "If he's able to talk, you mean. Leave him to us, boss. Right, guys, who wants to be first?"

"Fuck off! I'm warning you, lay one finger on me—"

"Fond of repeating yourself, ain't you? You've had your chance, and time is getting on." Dave started laughing, making all his colleagues wonder what he was up to, including Kayli, who had stopped mid-stride on her way to question Michele in the back of the car. "I've just had a thought, guys. If he thinks us beating the crap out of him for resisting arrest will be bad, I wonder what his take will be when he gets transferred to prison. You know how the other crims love to punish paedos. Last one I heard about, three inmates strapped a paedo down and performed surgery on him without the assistance of anaesthetic."

"Wow, I didn't hear about that. What happened?" the constable holding Freeman's right arm asked, playing along with Dave's scare tactics.

Freeman's gaze darted between the two men.

Dave pointed down at his crotch and crossed his legs. "They cut his meat and two veg off, boiled it up, and forced him to eat them for his supper."

"What the fuck! You lot are sick if you think I'm going to fall for this shit," Freeman blustered, his eyes wide with fear in spite of his bravado.

"You needn't worry about that, though. We're going to give you the pasting of your life, and it'll be touch and go if you serve time anyway. Take him off the road over there, guys."

The constables pulled Freeman in the direction of a small wooded area.

The criminal dug his feet into the ground and leaned back. "You can't do this."

Dave shoved his hand in the youth's back, forcing him to stand upright, and whispered in his ear, "We can, and we will. And don't bother praying, either. God appreciates us carrying out a bit of discipline when it comes to scum like you."

Kayli watched the four men move slowly towards the wooded area. Then she turned and opened the back door of the car and slid in beside the girl. She winked at Graeme, who was listening to the feedback from the circulating chopper over the car radio. "Hello, Michele, I've been hearing an awful lot about you from the Watsons and the Halls, and I have to say, what they told me will be quite damning in the case against you when it reaches court." Michele's head sank onto her chest, and Kayli saw droplets fall from her eyes. "Crocodile tears don't wash with me, girl. If you want to redeem yourself, you're going to have to tell me where the children are and the names of the other people involved."

"I didn't mean to do it. It seemed like fun at the time, an easy way to earn some money."

"Fun! Terrorising the crap out of little girls? Murdering them? Are you as sick as you sound right now? Don't bother answering that—it was a rhetorical question."

"I didn't want to kill the girls. I was against that. Karl did it. I'm not going to have that charge laid at my door."

"Okay, I'll take that into consideration once we're back at the station. Something that will go in your favour also is if you tell us where the kids are being held. We know it's around here somewhere.

It's only a matter of time before the chopper locates them. Tell us now, and I'll make sure the CPS know how much you've cooperated with us."

Michele wiped her cheeks then her dripping nose with her sleeve as she contemplated Kayli's deal. Then she shook her head. "Karl said you'd try to bargain with us if ever we got caught and then back down on that deal. I'm not falling for that trick."

"Hey, it suits me..." Kayli stopped talking and listened to the crackling coming through the radio. "Turn it up, Graeme. Did he just say what I thought he did?"

"Sounds like they located a cottage, boss."

Kayli punched the air and smiled at Michele's petrified expression. "Looks like all the deals are off the table for you and your fella. The pair of you, and anyone else involved in this, are going to get what's coming to you after all."

Michele hitched up a shoulder and sneered. "Whatever, like I give a shit!" The meek and mild tone she'd been using moments earlier had turned harsh and full of anger.

"Maybe I should follow my colleague's stance and take you into the wooded area, as well, and make out you resisted arrest at the same time."

Michele's eyes widened in fear.

"Nah, you know what? On second thought, I'd rather not dirty my hands on filth like you. You'll get what you deserve from your fellow inmates soon enough." Turning to Graeme she said, "Take the two suspects back to the station with the other officers. Get them signed in and banged up in a cell. I'll question them tomorrow."

"With pleasure, boss."

Kayli left the vehicle and walked towards the group of four men coming out of the woods. Karl had blood dripping from one of his nostrils and a cut above his right eye. "We've located the cottage, guys. Can you do the honours and return to base with Graeme while Dave and I meet up with the chopper team?"

"Okay, ma'am."

"You ain't found nothing. This is just another ploy to get info out of me. Well, I ain't falling for it." Freeman smirked defiantly.

"Get him out of my sight before I do something I'll regret."

Kayli and Dave rushed to the car. Dave slipped behind the steering wheel and turned to face her. "Where is it?"

She pointed at the lane where the van had been disabled. "Can we squeeze past it? Looks like the cottage is up here after all."

"I'll do my best."

In the end, Dave went closer to the hedgerow to get past the vehicle and immediately put his foot down. Within seconds, Kayli saw the chopper circling overhead. Dave flashed his lights, letting them know he was on his way.

Kayli had an idea and fished her mobile out of her coat pocket. "Donna, it's me. We've got Freeman and Granger. Graeme is ferrying them back to the station to process them now. We're approaching a cottage where we believe the kids are being held. I need you to find out who owns this cottage. It's on Chancery Lane. Should be easy enough, looks like it's the only cottage out here."

"Leave it with me, boss. I'll get back to you ASAP."

Kayli ended the call. "What if it turns out to be the wrong location?"

"I hope to Christ it isn't. I fear what's going to happen to the kids if the main two looking after them are banged up in our cells."

"What about requesting an armed response team?" Dave suggested as he slung the car round a sharp corner.

"Steady, Dave. I want to get there in one piece. My gut is telling me that we won't need a team. Let's assess the situation when we get there and then decide."

The chopper seemed to be virtually overhead now. "Here it is."

Kayli opened the door and was running towards the cottage before Dave had even drawn to a halt. "Wait for me, boss."

The front of the cottage was overgrown. It didn't take a genius to work out that the gang had used the rear to access the building. She tore through the gate at the side and arrived at the back door. It was locked. She shoulder-charged it but immediately rebounded off the wood.

"Damn. Hurry up, Dave. I need your brute strength," she shouted.

Dave came to a screeching halt beside her, took a few steps back, and charged at the door. It gave under his combined strength and weight.

The kitchen was a tip and smelt of takeaways. Something caught her eye that made her heart skip several beats. Temporarily unable to speak, she pointed at a door off to the right.

Dave nodded. "It's a cellar. Want me to go first?"

Kayli fought hard to keep her emotions in check. Her eagerness to see if the children were down there and safe was constricted by the thought of finding a bunch of dead bodies lying in the creepy room beneath the house. Her phobia of confined spaces was also playing a part in her mind's decision-making process. "Yes, you go first."

Dave rubbed her arm and squeezed it gently. "Now don't you go breaking down on me."

"Ignore me. Go, Dave."

The door wasn't even locked. No light turned on when Dave flicked the light switch. He used the torch on his mobile to guide his descension into the smelly abyss. He stormed down the stairs and shouted, "Kayli, I've got them. They're all alive."

Kayli buried her head in her hands and openly sobbed, thankful that someone—or something—had guided them to the location before it was too late. "Thank God, Dave. I'll ring for back-up." Before she had a chance to make the call, her mobile rang. "Donna, Donna, we've got the children," she shouted emotionally.

"That's excellent news, boss! What a bloody relief."

"Get back-up over here right away. Call an ambulance, as well. They've been kept in a cellar. I have no idea if any of them are injured at this point."

"I'll do it right away, boss. I have some good news that I hope will be the icing on the cake."

Kayli's breath caught. "You've got the name of the person who owns the cottage?"

"I have."

Donna revealed the name. *Shit! Shit! Shit!* "Okay, Dave and I will shoot over there as soon as we're finished here."

"Don't you want me to send someone to pick up the suspect?"

"No. I want that satisfaction myself, Donna. Good work."

## 18

When the girls all surfaced from the cellar, Kayli hugged them one by one. "You're safe now, sweethearts. You'll be reunited with your parents shortly, I promise you."

The three girls were dumbstruck, squinting from the brightness of the daylight emerging through the window and back door. One of the girls ran to the window and looked out. There was nothing to see but an overgrown wilderness of a back garden, but Kayli knew the girl was embracing her freedom.

Kayli walked towards her and placed a gentle arm around her shoulder. The girl flinched at her touch. "It's all right, little one. No one will ever harm you again."

The girl turned and buried her head in Kayli's stomach. "I thought we'd never hear the birds or see the sun ever again." She started to sob.

Kayli looked over her head at Dave, and the pair of them wiped away their own tears.

The back-up team of Social Services, the paramedics and a team of uniformed officers arrived at the cottage within twenty minutes.

"We need to get out of here." Kayli pulled Dave's arm, but he was reluctant to leave the girls. "Dave, nothing is going to happen to them. Come on, we need to go."

"Where? You haven't told me where?"

Kayli held her hands out for the keys to the car. "Get in. You'll see soon enough."

Dave growled. "I hate it when you do that."

Kayli chuckled, which helped to relieve the tension in her shoulders. "I know you do. That's why I said it."

As they drove back through the country lane, she sucked in a breath and leaned over the steering wheel as she squeezed past the van blocking the route, clipping the bumper on the van's wheel arch in her haste. "Get onto the SOCO recovery service and tell them to get their arses into gear to shift that damn vehicle."

"Women drivers," Dave muttered before placing the call.

His dig earned him a thump on the thigh. Kayli impatiently flicked on the siren, eager to reach their destination swiftly. She switched it off when they were a few minutes away from their destination.

Dave's face was a picture when they arrived. He turned to her with an eyebrow raised.

She tapped the side of her nose. "You'll find out soon enough."

"I wasn't going to ask."

"Good."

Kayli spoke into the intercom system to gain access to the property then marched through the entrance and up the narrow corridor. She threw open the door, and a startled gaze met hers. "Dave, arrest him. Mr. Briggs, you really shouldn't have made that call dobbing in your associates."

Kayli heard the click-clack of heels come to a stop in the hallway behind her.

"What's the meaning of this intrusion, Inspector? You can't just march in here willy-nilly. We have a school to run."

"Do you want to tell her, Mr. Briggs? Or shall I?"

He had the decency to hang his head in shame. "I think we should all take this conversation elsewhere. My office perhaps?"

The head turned on her heel, expecting the three of them to follow her. Kayli motioned for Briggs to go ahead of her and Dave.

Dave leaned over and whispered, "He fooled me."

*The Missing Children*

"Me too, but no longer."

The head disappeared in her office, but instead of Briggs turning into the office, he bolted for the main entrance. "Another paedo who chooses to resist arrest," Dave shouted as he gave chase.

Kayli ran after the two men. Dave caught up with Briggs in the playground and held his head under his arm. Briggs tried to strike out at Dave, but the sergeant bopped him twice on the nose.

"Please, not in front of the children," Mrs. Laughlin shouted from the main entrance.

"She's right, Dave. Not here. We'll get our chance to avenge the children back at the station."

"I don't know what this is all about, but you're mistaken." Briggs desperately tried to protest his innocence, but it fell on deaf ears.

Dave hauled him back to the main entrance and forced him to stand in front of Mrs. Laughlin. "Tell her."

Briggs's lips remained tightly shut.

"What are they talking about, John? I demand to know."

Kayli stood alongside Briggs and Dave. "This man has been running a paedophile ring, Mrs. Laughlin. He's behind the abduction of Jamillia Watson and quite a few other children in the area. How many? I fear we will never know the exact number."

Eyes blazing and her fists clenched, Mrs. Laughlin stepped closer to the teacher. "Is this true?"

His chin dropped onto his chest. It was all the response the headmistress needed. Her hand flattened, and she slapped him hard around the face. "You, despicable excuse for a human being. How could you? May God strike you down for what you've done to those children." She looked at Kayli. "You should have told me. I wouldn't have stopped your partner had I known. May you rot in hell, you bastard." She ran through the hallway, then a door slammed.

"I think you've pissed her off, don't you? We've got the children, by the way. They're all safe. We've also got your accomplices in this heinous crime. I'm going to make sure you all go down for a very long time. You have my word on that. My team have worked tirelessly to hunt you down, but in the end, it was your stupidity that led us to your cottage. Did you really think we wouldn't be able to trace the deeds back to you?"

"I have friends in high places. You have no idea how far this goes, Inspector. I'll be walking the streets within a few weeks."

"Still talking bullshit, Briggs. Not with a couple of murder charges against you."

"I had nothing to do with the murders. That was down to Freeman."

"Tell it to someone who cares, arsehole. It's one of many charges we'll be filing against you. Put him in the car, Dave."

Kayli watched her partner tuck the paedophile into the back of the car. Someone knocked on a window nearby. Kayli looked to see who it was and saw dozens of relieved faces smiling at her. Briggs's pupils. They raised their thumbs and mouthed "thank you" in unison. That one satisfying gesture would stay with her for the rest of her life. Over the coming weeks, she sensed all his pupils would come forward to share their experience of abuse at the hands of their teacher, putting an extra nail in the evil man's coffin.

# EPILOGUE

Over the next few days, interviewing all the suspects remained Kayli's priority. To her delight, having the three of them in custody worked in the team's favour as Briggs, Freeman and Granger were all keen to inform on their partners in crime, showing very little loyalty towards each other.

Each suspect's home was searched, and their computers were sent to the forensic lab to be examined. Naomi had discovered numerous files with names and addresses and several emails to one particular person that referred to the transportation of the girls out of the country in a week's time. Kayli felt relieved that things had slotted into place before the girls had left British shores. Briggs's contact was known to Vice for suspected prostitution and human trafficking, but they had yet to find the evidence to present to arrest the man. Kayli passed on the information Naomi had uncovered, and Jordan Somers was immediately arrested.

Kayli had a feeling she would be dealing with the case for a few more weeks in light of the names found on Briggs's computer. There were some pretty influential people on the fringes of the crime that she and her team would enjoy bringing to justice. One thing Kayli couldn't figure out was why Freeman had killed the children. After hours of interrogation he finally admitted that every time he looked at Jamillia he saw Michele having sex with Kelvin Watson, he needed to rid himself of that image. As to killing Sophie, his logic was unbelievable, he said he didn't like the way the girl looked at him, so punished her. Proving what a sick, twisted individual he really was. Another snippet of information came via Marcia Watson, who had confided in her parents that Michele Granger had abused both her and her sister. She had revealed that when Michele used to babysit them, she often gave them cold baths and frequently struck the soles of their feet with a wooden spoon.

~

It had been a very busy week, and Kayli had neglected Mark the past few days, but on Saturday, they spent a leisurely morning in bed together. Giles had been dropping hints for days that he would have good news to share with Mark at the family barbeque.

Kayli slapped him on the backside. "Come on, you, we better get moving. You know how Mum hates anyone being late. I promised to help with preparing the salads."

Mark groaned and rolled over again while she jumped in the shower.

An hour later, they arrived at her parents' detached house on the edge of town. It was a beautiful September day; no hint of a cloud to spoil their enjoyment. Giles was already there with Annabelle and their two-year-old son, Bobby. Mark made a beeline for Giles, hoping to hear some news, but Giles shoved a can of beer in his hand and told him to be patient.

Sensing Mark's frustration, Kayli was keen to get away from him. She walked into the house and found her mum and dad in the kitchen. Her mum, as usual, was tearing around as if possessed, shouting orders at her father, who seemed torn in which direction to go first.

"Mum, calm down. Tell Dad clearly what you need him to do, then give me a job."

Moira Bright stood still and sighed heavily. "I'm sorry. I just want this day to be a success. It's not often I get to have my whole family around me."

Kayli hugged her. "We neglect you, and I'm sorry. Life gets in the way a lot, too much really. It doesn't mean that we don't think about you."

"I know, dear. All right, less panic and more action. Can you make the Jamie Oliver dressing for the salad? His book is on the counter next to all the ingredients. All you have to do is mix them all together."

"No problem."

"Ron, you need to take the meat out to the barbeque area. You can start cooking it now that everyone is here."

"Yeah, you do that, Dad. I'll help Mum prepare the rest of the food and start ferrying it out when it's ready."

Within an hour and a half, they had prepared, cooked, and were working their way through the mountain of food her parents had laid on and getting merry on the alcohol Giles was plying them with.

She grabbed her brother's arm as he passed on his way to obtain more supplies from the house. "When are you going to put Mark out of his misery? You're not being very fair, love."

"Soon. Let me top up everyone's glasses, and then I'll announce it."

Kayli pecked her brother on the cheek. "Thanks for everything you've done, Giles."

"I'll do anything for you, sis. You know that."

Kayli moved closer to Mark, who was playing with Bobby on the lawn. For some reason, her stomach was tying itself in knots.

Giles emerged with a couple of bottles of champagne and a tray of clean glasses. "Gather around, folks. Let me pour the plonk, and I'll share the good news I have."

Mark rushed to Giles's side, and as he poured the champagne, Mark handed around the glasses.

"Everyone, I'd like you to raise a glass to help me celebrate Mark getting his new role as head of security."

Mark and Kayli stared at each other.

Giles laughed. "Well, give your man a kiss, sis. This job is huge."

"Security? Where? What company?"

"Ahh… that's the sixty-four-thousand-dollar question. Mark, I hope your passport is up-to-date."

"What? It's abroad?" Kayli screeched.

Mark nodded. "I renewed it last year. Where is the job based, Giles?"

"It's based here in the UK, but our first job—yes, I'll be going with you—is in Afghanistan."

Everyone fell silent, their gazes flitting around the group. Kayli looked at Annabelle and tilted her head as if to ask, "Did you know about this?"

Annabelle shook her head, slammed her glass on the table, lifted her son in her arms, and stormed into the house. Giles watched her go, his mouth hanging open.

"You can be so dumb at times, Giles. Why didn't you run this past us before making the grand announcement?"

"Hey, come on, sis. This is a fabulous opportunity, and the money is huge."

"As well as the risk of being killed, no doubt."

"Mark? How do you feel about it, mate?" Giles slapped Mark on the back.

Kayli turned her head sharply, eager to hear his response.

He shrugged and grinned. "The money side of things sounds good."

"Are you kidding me? What about the risks?"

"That was never a concern to you when I was in the army, love. I can't see what the issue is."

After that she decided to keep quiet, not keen on making a fuss in front of her parents. If Mark accepted the post, she was unsure whether their relationship could, or should, continue. Giles, in trying to do something good in his life, had possibly destroyed all their lives in the process.

## THE END

Thank you for reading THE MISSING CHILDREN; I sincerely hope you enjoyed reading this book as much as I loved writing it.

If you liked it, please consider posting a short review as genuine feedback is what makes all the lonely hours writers spend producing their work worthwhile.

Don't forget there are a further five books plus a fast-paced novella in this series. You can get the next book here **Killer on The Run.**

# KEEP IN TOUCH WITH THE AUTHOR

Newsletter
http://smarturl.it/8jtcvv

BookBub
www.bookbub.com/authors/m-a-comley

Blog
**http://melcomley.blogspot.com**

Join my special Facebook group to take part in monthly giveaways.

**Readers' group**

Printed in Great Britain
by Amazon